BOOKS BY AVA STRONG

REMI LAURENT FBI SUSPENSE THRILLER
THE DEATH CODE (Book #1)
THE MURDER CODE (Book #2)
THE MALICE CODE (Book #3)
THE VENGEANCE CODE (Book #4)
THE DECEPTION CODE (Book #5)
THE SEDUCTION CODE (Book #6)

ILSE BECK FBI SUSPENSE THRILLER
NOT LIKE US (Book #1)
NOT LIKE HE SEEMED (Book #2)
NOT LIKE YESTERDAY (Book #3)
NOT LIKE THIS (Book #4)
NOT LIKE SHE THOUGHT (Book #5)
NOT LIKE BEFORE (Book #6)
NOT LIKE NORMAL (Book #7)

STELLA FALL PSYCHOLOGICAL SUSPENSE THRILLER
HIS OTHER WIFE (Book #1)
HIS OTHER LIE (Book #2)
HIS OTHER SECRET (Book #3)
HIS OTHER MISTRESS (Book #4)
HIS OTHER LIFE (Book #5)
HIS OTHER TRUTH (Book #6)

DAKOTA STEELE FBI SUSPENSE THRILLER
WITHOUT MERCY (Book #1)
WITHOUT REMORSE (Book #2)
WITHOUT A PAST (Book #3)

PROLOGUE

Alison Beswick felt far too exposed out here, all alone. Strange things happened in the desert at night. To make matters worse, her feet ached from the three-mile trek. She shivered faintly, wishing she'd opted for a jacket, or even a sweater in the Nevada night. Now, though, on the side of the road, still marching resolutely forward, her backpack over one shoulder, she let out a shaking exhale. The lonely, desolate highway meandered through the deserts of Nevada. Miles of empty land and craggy mountains surrounded the long stretch of open road. Vegetation came sparse, clumped together in hues of mottled brown and pale green.

Briefly, she shot a look over her shoulder, catching a gust of chill wind. Alison stared back in the direction of the gas station.

She could no longer see it over the incline.

Could no longer glimpse the dim, neon sign, nor her equally dim boyfriend and his stupid Ford F-150.

Ex-boyfriend, she reminded herself, wincing and rubbing at the bruise forming beneath her cheek. She'd finally mustered the courage. Easiest diet ever—lost two hundred pounds of dead weight in one evening. All it had taken was a quick dose of honesty, bracing against a coward's punch, and a hasty sprint away from the parked truck.

"Shoulda dumped his ass years 'go," she muttered to herself, shaking her head and causing her shoulder-length brown hair to swish.

But even words, out here, seemed lost in the wind. She continued marching gamely forward, dust and stray strands of gravel from cracked road surfaces crunching beneath her feet. A soul, like those words, could get lost out here in the open desert, watched only by star-dappled skies and a chill wind.

Just then, behind her, she heard a faint growl. She scowled, turning sharply again, bracing for a moment.

She'd heard coyotes and mountain lions often lurked along these desolate stretches of road, near the mountains. Thoughts of sharp teeth and claws cutting through the thin fabric of her shirt sent shivers down her spine, accompanying the frigid prickles from the breeze.

But as the sound drew nearer, she tensed further, slowing and turning fully now to face the incline at her back.

An engine.

Rapidly approaching.

Her heart leapt briefly, in terror. Was he coming after her?

No... no, the engine was too small. Her ex's truck didn't just compensate in size, but also in sound. This new approaching vehicle wasn't pursuing her...

In fact, her eyes narrowed as she stepped onto the asphalt, her toes against the faded white line of paint. Her hand unclasped at her side and tremored beneath the still moon. She huffed, faintly, the bruise on her cheek aching.

"Come on," she muttered to herself. "Just a bit more courage..." Then, suddenly, she raised her hand, jutting her thumb up. Her eyes flashed in sudden exhilaration. In one day, she'd dumped her ex and now here she was, Alison Beswick, hitchhiking. She wondered what her old high school friends would say now. At twenty-one years of age, she hadn't had much chance to explore the world. But all of that was about to change.

She couldn't hold back the faint smirk dimpling her cheeks now as she raised her thumb aloft at the side of the road. Soon, as she stared in the direction of the asphalt incline, she spotted the glare of headlights coming over the hill. A second later, the grumbling engine manifested in the form of a rapidly approaching motorcycle. A low-rider, handlebars jutting like angry elk horns on the verge of charging.

She huffed in frustration, slowly lowering her hand, but as she did, almost in tandem, the biker pulled over to the side of the road, coming to a slow halt.

Dust swirled about, and Alison coughed, waving a hand in front of her face. In the dim light of the night, aided by the glare of the cyclops headlight beaming from the low-rider, she examined the biker hesitantly and swallowed.

A dark helmet, shaped and slick like a bowling ball. The visor low, also dark. The man didn't remove his helmet, didn't even look at her, just sat astride his bike, gloved hands on the handles. He revved the engine, exhaust spewing, but remained motionless, waiting.

Alison took a shaky step back from the painted line, staring at the odd silhouette. The man didn't move. Just waited. Sitting stationary. She swallowed and stared at the bike. Was he expecting her to hop on?

"H—hello?" she said.

The man gazed ahead, still not looking at her. She wasn't even sure it *was* a man. He had biker leathers, gloves, and a tinted helmet. For all she knew, he was just an empty shell with an outfit. Still, that would make him twice the man her ex had been.

"H-hi," she tried again, waving. "Umm, mind if I get a ride?"

Another rev of the engine. She admired his determination not to glance in her direction. He just sat perched on his bike, waiting, his headlight glaring across the dusty road. The distant mountains, the open desert terrain seemed even more isolating all of a sudden.

She glanced back again in the direction of the gas station. Still not visible.

She hesitated, her teeth pressing together. "I... I just need to find a motel... or something," she said carefully. "I can't pay you."

He didn't remove his helmet. Didn't move. Didn't speak. Not that it mattered; she wouldn't be able to hear him over the growl of the engine anyway. Quiet and stoic was preferable in many ways.

The chill lingered on her exposed arms, sending more prickles across her skin and helping her reach a conclusion. She couldn't just stand on the side of the road. Couldn't walk much further either. Her feet were already hurting. Besides, what if her ex came by in that stupid truck of his? No telling what he'd do if he discovered her alone on the side of the road...

Well. That wasn't entirely true. She knew exactly what he'd do.

"Thanks!" she said suddenly, lurching forward and pressing a hand to the back of the bike. Her fingers touched warm leather. The man still didn't move, just waiting, his shoulders hunched.

Tentatively, she reached out, pressing fingers against the quiet guy's leather jacket. She'd met shy guys before—in fact, she preferred them. The shy ones didn't always feel the need to push women around. She wished her boyfriend had been more shy. Now, she anchored herself on his shoulder and threw a leg over the bike, straddling the seat. Wincing, as if lowering onto a block of ice, she finally reclined in the seat and let out a faint little breath of relief once she was perched, her hands resting delicately on the man's shoulders.

He didn't tense. Didn't react. Didn't seem perturbed or interested or anything in between.

Suddenly, he pulled his feet up, throttled and began to pick up speed, spitting dust as he left the side of the road and took to the asphalt.

Alison didn't want to at first, but slowly she tightened her grip on the man's shoulder, wind picking up. She ducked her head behind the man's helmeted dome, using him as cover against the rising breeze.

Faster, faster, they sped forward.

Her legs braced against the metal shape of the rocket. Her heart had migrated somewhere near her throat. Her fingers tightened against the man's leather jacket as she held on for dear life. She'd never been much for motorcycles before. Still, all she had to do was hold on. How hard could it be?

"Thank you!" she tried to say, but the words were lost in the rising wind and the growling engine. She winced as her hair whipped about her face and her clothing pressed with the wind. Her fingers ached from where they tensed.

Faster, faster, the man was picking up speed. She tried to peek over his shoulder at the speedometer but found that the buffeting wind made this nearly impossible. She winced against the air current, ducking once more.

Faster.

Her stomach twisted. Maybe... maybe this had been a bad call.

She found her legs also tensed, one of them starting to form a cramp from the odd, tightened, and unfamiliar braced form. The hot metal of the bike beneath her was now warming her legs. Still, the man was increasing his speed. She wasn't sure she'd ever gone this fast before.

"Hey!" she tried to protest.

But again, the sound was lost. A lot could be lost out here, in an empty place like this. No one would hear a scream for miles in any direction. Hell, no one would hear a scream a foot in front of her due to the engine and the wind.

She tried tapping the man's shoulder urgently. Even this was a venture in courage as it required her to remove one hand in order to try and catch the driver's attention.

Tap. Tap.

Then he caught her hand and yanked.

Her stomach lurched, her eyes widened, she screamed but the sound was lost once more.

He pulled her hand off his shoulder and wrapped it around his waist. She tried to yank her hand back, but his gloved hand tightened, gripping her fingers *hard.*

"Stop!" she tried to scream. "Let me off! Let me go!"

But the speed only increased. His grip only tightened. She was now racing through the heart of a Nevada night on an abandoned road, her hand clamped in the driver's grip.

No way off. No way to stop. No escape.

CHAPTER ONE

Dakota Steele frowned at the text message, re-reading it. *Got something I want to say. Coming over!*

Marcus was the last person she wanted to hear from. The FBI agent just didn't know when to leave well enough alone. What could he possibly want, anyway?

"Don't be stupid, Dakota," she murmured to herself. Of course, she knew *exactly* what he wanted. She'd been dreading this visit for months.

She slipped her phone back into her pocket, scowling and returning her attention to the task at hand.

Dakota held the watering can in a firm grip, watching in fascination as the liquid trickled in the pewter flowerpot. Momentarily, the phone and the ominous text was forgotten as she stared at the single jutting stem of the orchid. No flowers—she'd trimmed off the old, wilting branch at the second nub. It would regrow. That's what the online experts had said. But it had been two weeks, and nothing yet.

Still, she diligently watered the orchid, determined to see it through. As the plant itself took a drink, she joined it, throwing back the nearly empty beer bottle in her other hand.

The orchid would rebloom—it had to. The same couldn't be said for former BAU agent, Dakota Steele. Despite her old partner's best efforts.

She frowned at this thought, and slowly lowered the watering can. Marcus was a persistent man—she had to give him that. She glanced at the clock above the cramped apartment's small television set on the other side of the room, away from the window and the orchid. Five minutes until Marcus was supposed to show up.

She pulled her phone from her pocket, double-checking to make sure she hadn't received any new updates. But the last text message was the same. She scrolled past the first message towards the last one. *Be there in twenty-five.* Marcus was a punctual man.

She frowned at the presumption of the text. She'd never really been able to say no to her old partner. She didn't like speaking much either way. Words were... useful. To some. But words, in her mind, were simply preemptive to someone else solving one's problems. She'd never been given that luxury. She solved her own problems.

The screen saver on her phone was a reminder of this—an image of a black hexagonal cage. She'd spent years in that thing, training—fighting. The only pictures she had, which she'd framed herself, sat on the cabinet by the television. Each of them displayed images her father had taken—grainy, nearly a decade old. All of them showing a younger Dakota preparing for a bout or raising her hands in victory. She had some medals and even a couple of trophies, but these she kept locked beneath her bed. They gathered dust—what else would they be useful for? No reason to linger on past accomplishments.

The photos, though, were reminders. She particularly favored the ones where she'd gotten her ass kicked. Each of them a lesson. A lesson she thought she'd learned until three months ago.

Marcus or not, she wasn't going back to the FBI.

She took another long drink from her bottle and, once she was finished, walked over to the recycling can and gently lowered the glass into the container, shivering as she did. She glanced around her tidy apartment. Neat, organized. Even now, the fifth bottle deposited in the canister where it belonged. Already, she felt a healthy buzz.

Still, a little bit of chemical dependence and a lot of PTSD didn't mean she had to live like a slob. *Control the controllables*—wasn't that what her old coach always used to say?

She adjusted the watering can until it was symmetrical to the flowerpot and then began to check her phone again.

Tap. Tap.

She stiffened, shooting a look toward her door, eyes narrowed. She swallowed once, tasting the bitter tang of the sour draft.

Another insistent *Tap, Tap.*

She sighed but didn't say anything, blinking blearily and trying to clear her vision. She held her alcohol well enough. The knock on the thick, metal door—with the bolt and the chain—was too polite for the area. Things were done differently in Rapid City, South Dakota. She'd come home a few months ago, after...

After the incident...

She shivered in horror and looked frantically towards the six pack on the counter. Just the plastic rings left. She'd have to grab some more liquid courage from the fridge.

Tap. Tap.

Not now, though. Marcus would never let her hear the end of it. It had been only a few short months since she'd left the agency. Her wavering sobriety, though, wasn't nearly so new. She'd battled this particular demon for more than a decade.

"Hello?" a pleasant voice called through the door. "Dakota?"

She scowled again, jamming a trembling hand into her pocket. She adjusted the sleeves of her turtleneck. A neat, pressed shirt smelling of lavender. Her pants were creased and might have seemed less out of place on the form of a lawyer or a banker.

But like the tidiness of her place, Dakota liked presenting a certain front. Appearances mattered. Besides, the neat shirt and pants hid the tattoos. Some of them she still liked, but most were badges gifted by the stupidity of youth.

She reached the door, unlocked it, unlatched and opened it. Normally, back in the hood, she would double-check to make sure this was a guest she was expecting. A single woman, in her thirties, moderately attractive with sea-gray eyes—one could never be too safe. Granted, most good-for-nothings if they knew anything about her, or her past, would likely skip this particular apartment for their ill-intentions, but a girl could never be too safe.

She recognized the voice, however. A gentle, soothing tone. Like the voice of a doting father or a particularly compassionate youth pastor. Not that she'd been in a church in a long time.

As the door swung open, she rearranged her features. The scowl vanished; the pressed lips loosened. Appearances mattered.

She stood poker-faced, impassive in the doorway of her apartment on the bad side of town back in her old, childhood stomping grounds. She'd returned three months before, but the place fit like a glove. This was where she belonged.

The same couldn't be said for the lumbering galoot just outside her door.

"Galoot" was a word he'd taught her.

His size was second only to his immense vocabulary and his appetite for educating others on his pet favorite words.

Today, it seemed, was no exception, announced by the sudden clearing of his throat, a smiled greeting and then, "Angakkuq," he said simply.

Dakota quirked an eyebrow, absentmindedly touching her fingers to her turtleneck collar, making sure the tattoo of the dragon whose tail ended over her throat was hidden from sight. A nervous tic she'd developed over the years. Once upon a time, in her cage-fighting days, she'd displayed the tattoos proudly. Things had changed. So many things.

“Hmm?” the gentle giant asked, matching her quirked brow.

Dakota just shrugged.

“Angakkuq,” he said primly, adjusting his glasses, “is an Inuit wizard.”

She snorted. “Yeah right.”

“It's true,” Marcus insisted. “Look it up.”

“Don't gotta,” she replied. “I trust the brain that told me mundungus was a type of withered leaf.”

“Ah, tobacco actually,” he said, clearing his throat.

She nodded, but the motion was a bit delayed. The faint buzz in her skull had migrated to her lips, and she closed her eyes briefly, attempting to stave off a headache. Her mind felt looser, now, less taxed. The dark cloud from earlier, the one that had made it difficult to even rise from her bed was fading. Not gone, but somewhat forgotten, or veiled. The drink served as somewhat of an umbrella against the deluge. An umbrella made of tissue, though—it faded fast.

For the moment, though, Dakota was glad to simply be even keeled. She acknowledged Marcus Clement in her doorway. A tall, black man whose muscles barely squeezed into his comic-book t-shirt. A faint mustard stain had been rubbed from the upper pectoral, and she frowned at it, briefly, her more basic instincts screaming for orderliness.

The giant, muscled FBI agent looked like a Doberman, but really was a golden retriever. She wished she had a smile for him. But her lips hadn't found reason to curl for a long time now... Especially since...

She swallowed, her eyes staring off. A body. A dark room. A discarded purse stained with blood, the strap wrapped around her neck.

She wanted to grit her teeth, to squeeze her eyes or scrub them against the horrible images. But appearances mattered. So she kept her expression as guarded as ever.

“You look great,” he said conversationally. “As ever.” He glanced towards her eyes, and she wondered if he spotted the red rings, the dilated pupils. He rarely missed small details. But he glanced away the same way she had from the mustard stain on his comic-book t-shirt.

“Why are you here, Marcus?” she said, not one to mince words. “Not really a nice part of town for a social call.”

“It's...,” he glanced over his shoulder towards a railing with more than one piece of gum stuck to the dilapidated thing. “Quaint,” he said, turning back to her and forcing a smile. Mostly white teeth, a couple off-white. He hadn't brushed this morning. She pushed the thought from her mind. She noticed details, especially details about *people* and their appearances. Growing up, training as a ju-jitsu and kickboxing practitioner, she'd been raised in the school of thought in which focusing on one's opponent's weaknesses was just as important as focusing on one's strengths. *What you don't know, you can't defeat.* Her old mentor's favorite saying. The old Irish tough guy lived in the same town. Though she hadn't been by to visit since she'd returned.

Marcus rubbed at his chin. "Are you here alone?" he asked, trying to phrase it conversationally, but the concern in his tone was evident.

She frowned. "Yeah."

He waited for her to expound. But he knew her well enough not to wait *too* long. He sighed, shaking his head. "And your father? Does he still live in the area?"

She shrugged. "Don't even know if the house is still here. Marcus, again, what do you want?"

Now it was his turn to pause and allow the silence to linger. His throat tensed. His fingers tapped against his large thigh. His eyes flitted then steadied. She knew people. She knew their weaknesses, and their strengths. She'd spent a lifetime studying others. As a woman in the fight game, half the battle was gaining an advantage wherever it could be found. She'd competed with other women in the cage, but more than one man—trying to prove some testosterone-fueled point to a buddy at the time—had picked a fight with her after a match, or at a bar, or just for the fun of it.

Information was advantage. Knowledge meant knockout.

And she *knew* what he wanted even without him saying anything. The way he hesitated, the faintly guilty look in his eyes replaced by a stern posture of defiance as if resenting his own guilt. Also, she spotted the rolled-up folder in his baseball-glove-sized right hand.

"That a case?" she asked, pointing.

Instinctively, he flinched, his hand jerking back nearly imperceptibly. He caught the motion though and just let the rolled folder remain jutting.

"It is," she said. It wasn't a question. Her expression remained emotionless, but inwardly her chest tightened. She needed to grab another drink but didn't want to partake in front of Marcus. Her head was pounding now. "Why are you on my doorstep with another case?" she said, her voice firm.

He sighed. "Look, Dakota, please, hear me out."

She considered this. Then shook her head. "Nah. Nice seeing you, Marcus." Then she shut the door. As it swung shut, though, an economy-sized foot jutted in the doorway. Just as quickly it jerked back. "Sorry, sorry," he said quickly. "Sorry," he repeated. He winced and adjusted his spectacles. "Look, Dakota, I wouldn't be here if it wasn't important. Please, please hear me out. For old time's sake, yes?"

"There a word for that?" she said. "Old time's sake?"

"Er... Commemorative?"

"Nice." She shut the door again.

This time he didn't try to interrupt.

She turned, moving back towards the fridge.

Tap. Tap. More insistent this time. "Dakota!" A muffled voice called through the door. "Please—we all want you back. I want you back. This won't be like last time."

She flinched, having reached the fridge now, one hand gripping the cool handle of the appliance. She didn't reply, preferring her silence. She opened the fridge, scanning the contents. More beers. A bottle of ketchup, a packet of soup and milk that looked like sludge...

She sighed. She'd have to go to the store soon enough.

Tap. Tap. "I don't blame you!" the voice echoed through the door. "I never did."

She tensed at this, turning. Now that no one was watching, she allowed the scowl to curdle her features, and she directed it towards the door. She touched her fingers towards her turtleneck again, just to make sure it was still there.

"Anyone could have made that mistake!" the voice continued. It waited as if expecting a response. When none came, with a huff, it continued, "Anyone! I wasn't even sure about the lead myself. It was fifty-fifty."

Dakota snorted at this. Her partner was being generous, and he knew it. So did she. As a former agent, she'd worked with the BAU—closely examining threats for a living. But the last case, the one three months ago, had ended in disaster. And it had all been her fault. She'd let a killer escape, and a young girl die.

The same way it happened to Carol... A nasty voice whispered in her head.

She flinched at a far more distant memory of her own baby sister. Two decades was a long-time, but not nearly long enough to outpace certain recollections. She snatched a bottle from the fridge, twisted the non-twist cap with a heavily calloused hand and chugged the thing in four gulps.

The smooth, somewhat bitter drink assuaged her throat, wetting her lips. She walked over to the recycling and lowered the bottle into the trash.

Marcus had known she'd been wrong about the killer three months ago. Had offered another lead. He'd wanted to follow an anonymous tip. It had the markers of the killer. He'd probably been right, but they'd never know because Dakota hadn't been able to see clearly. The case was too close—had been too close to her own sister's death. It had clouded her judgment; she'd ignored her partner's lead and she'd single-handedly allowed a murderer to flee, a young girl to die...

She'd left the BAU the next day and returned home. Prior to that, she'd made a good agent. A damn good one, in fact. But that case... just too similar. Too much baggage.

"I flew here just to speak with you!" Marcus said, patient as ever. His voice didn't carry an inch of hurt or frustration. Only concern and a plea. "They're sending me west," he said. "My flight is this evening. From the Regional. You should come with me, Dakota! It's been long enough. I need you at my back."

"Get Spencer!" she called back, waiting for the newest drink to take its effect.

"Spencer's unideal," he retorted through the door.

"Is that how you pronounce asshole?" she called back.

The man on the other side of her door snorted. He didn't swear himself, but he often had a schoolboy reaction when others did. Just another reason she liked the guy. She wouldn't have even opened the door for anyone else from the agency. Now, though, she was wishing she hadn't made an exception. Not even for her old partner.

"Just think about it, alright?" he called through the door. "I need the backup, and I don't trust anyone else."

"The new boss feel the same way?" she called back, scowling at the door.

"Oh—you heard about her?"

"I heard there was some movement up top after my screw-up."

Marcus sighed. "That's good for you," he said, trying to keep his tone light. "No baggage. Maybe she doesn't even know you quit."

Dakota snorted. "Funny."

"Alright, maybe not. But this case is a serious one, Dakota. The women are young. Mid-twenties max. *Look*—can you do that? Just take a look?"

She heard a huff and then a grunt and then light moving beneath her door. A second later, the same rolled up folder she'd spotted was now being slid beneath the crack under the door. She frowned, watching the folder emerge in her living room.

The one thing in the tidy place now marring the carpet.

For this reason alone, she marched over, snatched the thing and moved straight towards the recycling bin, tossing the papers in without a second thought.

"Did...," the voice paused. "Did you just throw it away?"

"Yup," she called back.

"Really?"

"Uh-huh."

"Dakota... please. I need your help!"

"You're just saying that. I'm not going to, Marcus."

"This is no way to live!" the big man implored, despite the barrier in his face. "Alone in a rancid part of town..."

"I thought you said it was quaint."

"I lied."

Dakota snorted humorously. "I miss you too, Marcus. But I'm not coming back."

The shadow shifted beneath her door. The voice didn't reply at first. Briefly, she thought perhaps he was still lingering, but then she heard a sigh and the faint sound of retreating footsteps. Moments later, she heard the buzz of the door below.

Once more, she was alone.

Dakota frowned, her head buzzing, her gaze blurry. She turned to face the pruned orchid, staring at the naked plant. Marcus had been the one who'd bought the flower for her. A year ago. He'd thought it might make her happy.

Most things didn't make her happy. She wasn't even sure what the word meant.

But it had made her... grateful? Glad? As close to happy as she knew how to get. But now the flowers had wilted. Nothing had budded back.

She was alone again. But she sure as hell wasn't going to help on some new case. Wasn't going to let Marcus lure her back.

Suddenly, she heard a tapping sound against the window.

Dakota whirled around, staring past her orchid.

Another tap.

She frowned and hurried over, peering out across the street. She didn't lean out too far. A few seconds passed and she heard the downstairs door open and close. The big man, head bowed, moved up the street in the opposite direction.

Dakota didn't call after him.

Instead, she glanced towards a couple of kids with shit-eating grins.

They were standing in the big red dumpster, pebbles in their hands.

Dakota got one glimpse of the yellow t-shirts they were wearing, and her eyes narrowed. At the same time, she felt a jolt of fear.

Two reunions on the same day?

What were the odds? She frowned. Not high. Unless... unless Marcus was pulling strings.

But Marcus didn't scare her half as much as what the two kids heralded.

"Get lost!" Dakota called out, waving a hand. "Go!"

The kids tossed their pebbles in the trash can.

"He said you better be up!" One of the kids shouted, still grinning. "Said he's coming by."

Dakota rubbed at the bridge of her nose.

Those yellow shirts came from Little's gym.

Coach was stopping by. Shit. Had Marcus called him? Must have. She made a shooing motion again and slammed the window.

Coach always did have an unusual way about him. Pebbles on the window—like something out of a movie. He'd sent his two gym rats to keep an eye on her, no doubt. She felt like a bird in a cage, being watched.

Part of her considered bolting, making a break for it. If she wasn't home, he couldn't confront her, right?

Then again, those two kids outside were likely tasked with following her wherever she went.

More tapping against her window. More pebbles.

She sighed. They'd probably been assigned to keep her up. Keep her there.

Until Casper Little arrived. Like the godfather himself.

"Dammit...," she muttered. With Casper, one could never really tell what he was thinking. His little lookouts would keep an eye on her for as long as he told them. An hour? Six?

He might stop by at midnight or at the break of dawn the next day.

No telling with him, and Dakota wanted nothing to do with another surprise meeting on the same day. She felt like that little furry-footed creature from that movie she'd once seen. Habit? Hobo? Something like that.

Well... no naps with pebbles rattling off her window every five minutes. No time to relax knowing Casper was en route to her place either. She shivered at the thought of his temper when he realized she'd been in town for months without stopping by.

Suddenly, a horrifying thought struck her.

Marcus was more forgiving, but Casper would *smell* the beer on her.

"Shit," she muttered. "Shit. Shit... Dammit."

Another pebble bounced off her window.

How much time did she have before Casper showed up?

Not much. Not much at all. But hopefully just enough to cover her tracks.

She spun on her heel, racing down the hall.

CHAPTER TWO

Only ten minutes or so had passed since Marcus had left, and the pebble-throwers had shown up. Now, Dakota stood beneath the freezing cold spray from the shower head, hands raised in front of her. Her knuckles dusted one cheek; the other hand hovered at eye-line in front of her. Her shoulders squared, her legs angled, presenting as small a form as possible to a potential aggressor. The shower would wash the stink. The cold would rouse her.

Now, a bit more awake, awaiting the imminent arrival of the king of Rapid City, she found the tight confines of the shower the perfect place to practice her movements. At least something to keep her mind occupied. Given the freezing water, the slick tiles, the close quarters, it perfectly prepared for the hand-to-hand proximity of the cage.

Not that she'd had a professional bout in years.

Still, she loved the sport. Had always loved it.

Loved fighting in a way. Plus, the motions distracted her. Casper was gonna be pissed—no doubt about it. Three months without stopping by. She could picture that little vein bulging in his forehead already.

But no... No—he'd come when he came. Sometime soon. Or later tonight. Didn't matter.

Her muscles tensed; her jaw clenched. She shivered under the freezing spray. Jab. Jab. Uppercut. She shifted her stance, trying southpaw. Even on the slick ceramic, her feet were steady, her strong legs providing a sturdy base. Left, left, right, overhand left.

Her fingers grazed the dappled tile, barely missing. She kicked with her left, pivoting on the right. Her foot threatened to slip, but she adjusted her position last minute, maintaining her posture, maintaining her balance, and lowering her leg a second later.

She envisioned a counterattack, protecting her face, elbows tucked, hands raised, knuckles to forehead. Just like her old mentor used to teach her.

She lowered her hands suddenly, sealing her eyes and letting the frigid spray speckle her cheeks. She held her breath, still with her eyes closed. She could see images gouged into her mind's eye. Other, older images. Memories. Twenty-year-old, dusty, buried secrets.

Things she'd never discussed with anyone. Not Marcus. Not Casper. Not her father—damn, she hadn't seen the old man in years.

Things they knew, though. Everyone at the BAU had known.

The little bitch from South Dakota. A pity hire. That's what they'd whispered at the water cooler. That's what they'd thought. They hadn't seen the years she'd spent studying forensic science. She'd even gotten her GED after dropping out of high school senior year. All they saw were the hidden tattoos peeking from behind her sleeves and favored turtlenecks. They heard her rough patterns of speech that she failed to disguise when things got sharp. Half of them had blamed her for the death of that little girl months ago. If they hadn't hired an affirmative action case... Hadn't hired a dropout... After her GED, she'd gone on to college, but it had never felt quite right.

She'd heard their whispers. Some of them more like shouts.

She kept her eyes sealed, enjoying the blistering of the chill spray. Her head still buzzed from the beers. And yet she still had her balance. Still could focus.

But couldn't forget.

She pictured the small, cherubic, dimpled face of her baby sister, Carol. Six-years-old when she'd vanished. Six-years-old—two decades ago—when they'd found her bloody backpack. Sea-gray eyes in an angelic face stenciled on the inside of Dakota's eyelids, and she wanted to scream.

She burst into another series of practiced motions. Left, left, right, uppercut. Faster. Faster. Left foot, right. Right high kick. Showerhead knocked loose. Scream.

Reset.

Right, right—droplets flying—left through the bastard's evil face.

She screamed, slamming her fist into the tiled wall, throwing her body behind it.

A knuckle cracked. So did a tile.

She screamed again. Not in pain, but in defiance. In fury. Appearances mattered.
But not here. Not beneath the freezing spray. Her hand hurt now, throbbing. Didn't matter. To hell with pain. Pain was nothing.

Right, right, overhand right, knee—clinch. Release, distance. Space. Left high kick.

She nearly slipped this time. Her foot sliding on the slick ceramic. She breathed heavily, hands still raised, eyes still closed. Some things she didn't want to forget.

Sometimes, her little sister's memory was the only good thing she had left in her life. Carol's dimpled cheeks were always smiling in Dakota's mind. Always reminding her of better times.

Of course, Carol's death had been Dakota's fault as well. She'd gotten into a fight at school. Gotten into a fight and been held after. Hadn't been there to walk her baby-sister home. To protect her.

She screamed again. Flowing through another series of rapid motions in gelid wet.

And then she collapsed like a puppet with snipped strings. Partly slipping, partly allowing the motion to bring her painfully thumping into the bottom of the shower.

She sat there, her back throbbing, her skin trembling, freezing, her eyes sealed shut.

A faint whimpering moan leaked from her lips.

Pathetic, she thought to herself.

She was a fighter. A fighter—damn it! *Get up!* She screamed in her mind. *Get the hell up!*

But she remained seated in the curved shower basin, trembling and hyperventilating. Desperately wanting nothing more than for all of it to just stop. She felt like a little girl again, nursing a cut on the playground, waiting for a parent to come kiss it and make it better. Except, her father had never been the injury-kissing sort.

She slumped, head tapping against the back of the tub. Her hands trembled so badly in front of her, the one with the popped knuckle throbbing in pain.

Maybe she was overthinking it all.

A killer had gotten away three months ago, murdering a little girl. Another killer, twenty years ago, had also gotten away. That time leaving a more familiar child dead in his wake.

The center of it all had been Dakota.

The bodies of two little girls were enough to erode any conscience, but hers had suffered on the acerbic ministrations of corrosive self-hatred for decades now.

She was running on empty. She needed some fun. A fling. Something.

Suddenly, she heard a loud pounding from the direction of her living room.

Her eyes fluttered open, and she veiled her gaze against the water.

More pounding, joined by a voice this time. "I know you're in there!" shouted a voice she recognized. This one wasn't nearly so gentle as Marcus's had been. The loud fist wasn't nearly so polite. This voice, the fist, suited the area.

Fitting, because even from here, hidden in her shower, surrounded by the tapping droplets of a steady spray, she recognized the voice of Casper Little, her old kickboxing coach.

"Get your ass out here!" the rasping voice shouted. "Come on, Tastee!"

Tastee. She wrinkled her nose at the familiar nickname. A combination of the letters of her first and last name. Also, the name she'd fought under for years. Tastee. Tasty. A joke about how she liked the taste of blood.

A stupid joke, but Casper was ritualistic like that.

He was still bellowing as she wearily pushed off the slick ground, hands trembling, knuckle aching, and she regained her feet with a laden sigh.

She snatched a towel, kicked the faucet off and stumbled from the cramped confines of the space. Then, drying her hair, snatching her clothes, she took her precious time about getting dressed, making sure every button was done, every stitch of fabric in its proper place. She combed her hair, even as the pounding on her door continued, and only then, once she'd created a properly presentable spectacle, did she proceed from the bathroom and move with rolling footfalls towards the door.

She wasn't sure she was ready for this encounter.

Then again, she wasn't sure it was really up to her.

She flung open the door, this time, instead of easing it open, and stared from beneath hooded eyes, above a turtleneck collar, at the man standing in the door.

Hunched back, walking cane in one hand, liver spots visible on his old, worn, Irish skin. Casper had pale hair, like the ghost he was named after. He needed glasses according to his wife but refused to wear them. This had been the source of more than one fender bender in his time.

But most of the locals, most of the cops, most everyone had come through Little's Gym at some point in their life. Casper was something of a local legend.

Now, said legend was glaring at her from his squinting gaze.

"You look like right shite," he said, allowing some of the old country to bleed into his accent when expressing his severest displeasure.

“Hi to you too,” she muttered with a nod.

He snorted, shaking his head. Then, without an invitation, he stepped into her apartment, jostled roughly past her and moved into the kitchen.

“Hey!” she protested.

“Hey yourself,” he returned. He looked back at her, still scowling. Briefly, in the flicker of his eyes, she spotted a note of concern. A twitch of the lip, a faint misting of his gaze. She saw the compassion before he hid it completely.

Casper had always known how to best speak her language. He didn't take shit from anyone. Except, sometimes, Dakota. She'd always held a soft spot in his heart. Which was, partially, why she felt a surge of guilt at the way he was glaring at her. She'd been in town for months and hadn't visited.

“You been boozing?” he demanded, pointing his walking stick at her.

She crossed her arms. No sense in lying. It didn't sit well with her. Honesty had always been the best policy. Also, according to some, honesty was the first step to sobriety. Not that any program in that direction had ever stuck. “Yes,” she said simply.

He harrumphed. “Not any of the piss-water, yeah? At least you're nursing good stuff?”

She snorted in amusement, but just as quickly hid the expression, staring at her old coach. “Nice to see you.”

“Yeah? Feels nice. Feels real nice to hear you've been slumming for months but didn't stop by. I say something to hurt your feefees?”

“All the time.” She nodded. “Sir,” she added.

He grinned now, lowering the walking stick and pressing it against her carpet.

“Good to hear I'm not losing my edge,” he said with a laugh. “But I mean it, Tastee, you look like shit. Took me some time to find you, you know. Postman recognized you though.”

Dakota winced. “Snitch.”

“Guess you could say that. Could also say people in this town stick together. And I'm worried about you.” Again, his eyes flashed with that hidden compassion, that note of gentleness. Now, though, it took him a second to recover. He had missed a step in his old age. Looking at Casper, memories came flitting back. He'd been the father-figure she'd never had. Hell, he'd provided her a *home.* When she'd dropped out of school and spent some time couch-surfing, he'd taken her in. Seen her potential. How they'd met had been a story in its own right.

She had plenty of memories of the old man with the arthritic hands and liver spots. He no longer looked like the champion kickboxer she knew him to be. He didn't even look much like a gym owner. He just looked old. And kind—though this was hidden deep to those who didn't take the time to look.

"Nice of you to stop by," Dakota said. "I—I was going to say hi...," she trailed off, wrinkling her nose. "Didn't mean to snub you. Just had a lot on my plate." She shrugged one shoulder, her expression as devoid of emotion as ever. One thing could be said for Dakota Steele—she didn't cry easily. Didn't know how, really.

Now, her old mentor glared at her.

"Bullshit," he snapped. "Forget about me. You look like a mess. I can see it in your eyes, girl." He pointed his walking stick at her. "I can't stick around long. But it's worse than I thought. Hear me close, Tastee—you can't sit around moping alone in the dark, got it? Come by the gym. Or do something. Anything. Get the hell out of the house."

He wrinkled his nose and glanced towards the bulb-less orchid. "Dead plant," he observed. "Get some fresh air. Ton of flowers at the park."

Then, he spun on his heel, marched past her, pausing long enough to pat her on the shoulder and give a quick affectionate squeeze. Quieter as if worried someone might overhear, he whispered, "Really good to see you, Dakota."

And then, like the Irish whirlwind he was, he stepped back out into the hall. "I mean it," he called over his shoulder. "Ain't good for a soul to linger like you are. Good Lord didn't make us to hide indoors. Do something, Dakota! Anything!"

He waved an arthritic hand over his head in farewell and marched around the edge of the stairwell, curling down the steps and using his walking stick for leverage.

She watched him leave, frowning. Part of her wanted to call after him and say... say what? Anything, really. She didn't like being lectured without sticking up for herself. Then again, he had been her coach for years. Ten years ago, granted. But he looked pretty much the same. She knew she didn't. A streak of white graced her dirty blonde hair. A gift of pure stress.

Now, from the stairwell, she heard humming. A familiar tune—one of those old jazz numbers from the sixties that Casper liked playing around the gym.

She listened to the sound recede before closing the door again and standing still, facing the steel surface. One hand moved to the nearest chain, but she couldn't even summon the energy to attach it.

Maybe he was right. Maybe she needed to get out of the house. Do something.

What could it hurt?

A walk in the park?

But no—walking in any park locally was a good way to get mugged. A trip down to the gym? She wasn't sure she wanted to answer all the prying questions. *What brings you home? How was the East Coast? You were at the FBI? Why did you leave?*

She shivered at the horror of having to speak about herself.

No... no, maybe she had best just say in.

Or...

She glanced slowly over her shoulder towards the recycling bin. Her eyes narrowed.

Had Marcus and Casper colluded? Marcus was a manipulative son of a gun when he wanted to be. Her hands bunched instinctively at her side, but she winced at the injured knuckle and uncurled her fingers.

With a reluctant sigh, she marched over to the recycling bin, bent, and snatched the folder from the confines, opening it slowly.

Dakota stared at the front page. Her partner had removed the glossy images of the crime scene. She wondered if he'd done this on purpose, worried it might trigger an episode of PTSD. Or if he'd simply been sensitive to her current status as a civilian.

The BAU liked to keep things in house. Behavioral analysis didn't rest just with the killers and culprits. Colleagues also were subject to more than one theory about their own actions.

She scanned the printed pages carefully, reading at half the speed Marcus often managed. She had dyslexia, but her attention to detail meant she was perfectly capable of absorbing large amounts of information. It simply took her longer.

But her memory and ability to scrutinize more than made up for it.

She flipped the page, the paper crinkling along with her forehead.

"Motorcycle Murderer?" she read aloud, then snorted in disgust.

The pet nickname part of the job had never appealed to her. Call a spade a spade. A psycho a psycho. A murderer a murderer. Simple that way. Straightforward. No need to get cute with it.

She scanned the second page, scowling deeper.

A killer was out west... murdering women. In the deserts of Nevada on empty stretches of highway and in isolated locations.

No witnesses. No one had seen the murders, but people near the crime scenes—hikers and the like—reported the roar of a motorcycle engine around the time of each murder, before the bodies were discovered.

No real leads beyond that. No suspects for the moment.

I need you. I trust you...

Marcus's words haunted her nearly as much as Casper's.

She scowled now. They were *definitely* in collusion. She'd bet the box of medals beneath her bed that was the case.

She snorted, tossing the case file back in the recycling bin, this time with a bit more force. It lodged against one of her Coors Light receptacles.

She stared where it wedged, glaring at the offensive document.

She was done with that life. Done solving crimes.

Her buzz was fading, though. The emotions were slowly encroaching in, like the arrival of night itself. She shivered at the thought, hands tensed at her side. She wasn't sure what would happen when night fell. A few more drinks... Then what?

She wouldn't sleep. She hadn't slept well in months. The nightmares, the threat of anxiety... It was all also in collusion.

One way or another, she was surrounded.

At least in the case of Casper and Marcus, though, there was no talk of quick dives off tall bridges.

She stared towards the case file again, scowling.

Flight leaves this evening. Rapid City Regional Airport. That's what Marcus had said.

Of course, he'd said it. Just to lodge another little piece of self-doubt in her mind.

She let out a faint sigh, closing her eyes against a burst of a headache. Etched inside her eyelids, in her mind's eye, where hypnagogic imagery dwelt (another word from Marcus) she glimpsed the dimpled smile beneath sea-gray eyes.

"Dammit," she muttered. The women were young—Marcus had made sure to mention that point. Almost the same age her sister would have been if she'd made it into her twenties.

Could she really sit by, wallowing, while they were picked off by some leather-wearing biker dude? She'd spent time with that sort in the past, hadn't she? Her tattoos, her teen years... all of it. She knew the scene. Was that why Marcus wanted her? The age of the victims... He knew it would tweak her. The jerk.

She couldn't sit by. Not after reading the file. Why had she read the dang file? But no... Marcus had played his cards. Casper had followed up with the guilt trip.

Besides, it sure as hell beat a walk in the park.

She muttered darkly to herself, then snatched the folder from the recycling bin once again.

CHAPTER THREE

Of course, he'd texted her the terminal. The time. The flight number. She glared at her phone now, scowling towards the message from Marcus as her taxi pulled along the curb outside Terminal 3D. She'd packed light. Everything neatly folded, properly arranged, but compact, in the single carry-on luggage item she'd brought with her from New York when she'd returned home to her namesake state.

She gave a quick nod of gratitude, a quiet grunt, and a hefty tip to the man behind the wheel, then hit the curb jogging, glancing at her phone again.

Already ten minutes late. Dammit. She'd made up her mind but was going to miss the flight anyway. She picked up the pace, tugging self-consciously at her sleeves as she hurried through the sliding glass doors of the airport. Evening on a Wednesday night, nowhere near the holidays, allowed quick work through security, down the long, squeaking floors and to her indicated terminal.

As she hurried forward, carry-on clutched in the same hand with the popped knuckle, she frowned through the large, blue-tinted windows facing the tarmac.

The plane was still on the airstrip.

She frowned as she moved closer and spotted two flight attendants by the open door which led down the walkway towards the plane. Both of them looked up as she neared. "Agent Steele?" one of them asked.

She blinked, taken aback, unsure how to respond at first. "I—umm... Ms. Steele," she corrected.

The woman with the red scarf blinked but nodded politely. "Right—well, after you," she said, gesturing towards the ramp.

Dakota hesitated again, frowning as she did. Why had they been expecting her? Why was the flight still—

She suddenly loosed a shaking breath. Marcus. Of course. He'd used his connections to tell the plane to wait for her.

She felt a sudden surge of affection for her large, well-spoken compatriot, but just as quickly the emotion turned to resentment. He'd been very confident she'd join him.

Muttering darkly to herself, she allowed the attendant to guide her down the ramp towards the plane. She nodded in gratitude, murmuring, "Thank you," before moving down the spacious first-class seating, towards the indicated row 11, seat B of business-class.

What met her in the window seat was a beaming face with pearly teeth. Marcus grinned up at her as she hastily stowed her bag, trying to ignore all the attention directed towards her.

"Don't say a word," she muttered.

Marcus continued grinning.

She rolled her eyes, stowed her bag, and slowly fell into her seat, adjusting her shoulders against the familiar comfort of business-class seat padding. She liked flying. Most people liked complaining about airlines, but to Dakota, the whole thing was miraculous. She'd never been on a plane until her mid-twenties. Even her move east to study had been done in an old, run-down jalopy.

The idea of hurtling through the sky, far above, in the clouds, away from responsibility, requirements... away from everything. It was a miniature miracle.

She settled in her seat and heard the faintest *tap* next to her.

She glanced down and blinked.

Marcus's large hand was shielding the item he'd placed on the armrest between them.

"Figure you'd be needing this," he said in that same warm tone of his. He patted her arm, still shielding the item from view.

Her old service weapon in its holster, her badge clipped to the side. She let loose a shaky breath but nodded in gratitude and slipped the gun on the holster to her belt, using the clip-on metal clasps to secure it in place on her left hip.

She boxed southpaw but was good enough with both hands. An ambidextrous shooter, and fighter, she'd performed relatively well in most physical and marksman tests for the bureau.

The pilot's voice crackled over the speakers. A few of the other residents in business class were shooting Dakota reproachful looks, likely placing her as the source of their delayed departure.

She glanced towards Marcus who was still smirking. "You tell them to wait?" she asked.

He looked at her, his eyes twinkling like starlight.

Partly to wipe the grin off his face, and partly out of gratitude, she leaned in and planted a kiss on his cheek, complete with a loud smacking *mwah!* Sound.

Then, she leaned back in her chair, patting a shocked-looking

Marcus on his forearm. "Good man," she muttered. Then, in a much quieter tone, she added, "Thank you."

She shifted again, making sure the weapon was comfortable on her hip. The tarmac through the window began to move, the plane rumbling as it rolled onto the airstrip. The other passengers were no longer looking towards her. The flight attendant, ahead of them, moved through the motions, displaying safety measures.

"Did you read the file?" Marcus whispered once he'd recovered.

"Yeah. Nevada, right?"

"Hmm. We're meeting with the local sheriff. He's going to take us to the latest crime scene."

"Can't wait," she said, trying to put a brave face on it. But even at the words *crime scene* her stomach twisted. She felt like vomiting.

Was she really ready for this? Maybe she should have just gone for that walk in the park.

On one hip, she felt the weight of her handgun.

She stared at her hand—white and trembling on the armrest.

What if she wasn't ready? What if she was just going to ruin another case and lead to another death?

A sheriff would meet them. Take them to the next crime scene. Information gathering—that was all. Nothing was required of her yet. She could wait and see, couldn't she?

She'd wait to see the crime scene. It wasn't like she had another choice.

The plane began to rattle, picking up speed.

Her stomach was already twisted in knots by the time the wheels lifted off the pavement.

***

She inhaled the chill nighttime Nevada air as the sliding glass doors of the airport slid shut behind her. Standing on the curb, next to Agent Clement, the sheer size difference between the two of them was only further emphasized. Ahead, she spotted a silver SUV with a black grill pulling slowly to the curb.

A man behind the wheel peered out at them from beneath a neat, military haircut. He waved the two of them over.

"Agents Clement and Steele?"

"That's us," Marcus said cheerfully.

Dakota decided not to correct him this time. *Acting* agent. More a formality, really. Marcus may have returned her firearm, but she was just here the one time. That was it.

Even now, staring towards the silver SUV, her stomach twisted in knots. She wasn't sure why she'd agreed to this in the first place.

The two of them moved towards the parked sheriff's car. The doors clicked as they neared, and Agent Clement slid into the front seat out of sheer habit. Dakota, due to Marcus's size, had never resented allowing him the extra leg room of passenger side.

Besides, this way, sitting in the back, she wouldn't be expected to talk as much. She tugged at the sleeves of her jacket over her turtleneck and settled in the back seat which smelled of air freshener and stale cigarette smoke.

The pale-haired man in the front seat shot a look in the mirror, giving her a quick nod of greeting before gunning the engine and taking them from the curb, and away from the airport.

Marcus and the cop shared some pleasantries, but Dakota didn't listen, preferring to peer through the tinted window at the approaching terrain.

Plain land of Nevada. Long swaths of desert and mountains, cities linked only by highways. Dakota frowned across the expansive night, uninterrupted for miles as they left the airport, moving away from the glow of the city.

It was only as they picked up speed, moving onto a desolate highway, that she began to pay attention as Agent Clement was saying, "—and you mentioned a hitchhiker found the body?"

The sheriff nodded, shooting Clement a look. "That's right," he said. "Gonna be near forty-eight hours passed, but only just got the case. Passed on after a bit of a jurisdiction dispute."

Marcus nodded pleasantly. He always seemed to engage with people as if he actually *liked* them. Dakota didn't like nor dislike. She distrusted, and that was enough.

"Young woman," the sheriff was saying, his tone grim. "Not a local—still trying to ID her."

"I noticed that," Marcus replied. "She didn't have any ID on her?"

"None. Fingerprints being run, though. DNA too." The sheriff shrugged. "We're doing what we can. It's late—tomorrow labs open. Should have more then."

Agent Clement nodded politely. Dakota just sat in the back seat, wincing against a rising headache. She stared out the window, eyes on the dark blur of countryside as they moved through the western heart of

America, headed to find a corpse.

The drive passed in muted conversation from the front seat and sheer silence from the back. As they slowly pulled off the dusty road, Dakota perked at the glimpse of flashing blue and red lights illuminating the landscape ahead of them.

Two cruisers were blocking a rest stop entrance. She watched as a truck picked up speed, taillights flashing angrily as he moved on at the gestures of a deputy waving him forward.

"They found her on the side of the road," the sheriff was muttering as he moved past the stationed deputy into the rest stop. "Wasn't pretty."

Dakota leaned in now, her curiosity prompting a question. "Report didn't mention cause of death. Just said blunt-force trauma. Didn't detail."

The man glanced in the mirror again. "She was dragged to death."

Dakota frowned. "Dragged how?"

The man pulled the car to a halt, parking at the rest stop and twisted at the hips, watching her. "Dragged behind some vehicle, or a horse, or a motorcycle," he said.

"What, like alive?"

"When it started, yeah. Our killer is roping these women behind his bike and taking them for a ride. But that's only *after* he has some fun with them first."

"Fun? What sort of fun—torture?"

"That's the working theory. Deputy Peterson is waving me over. Looks like we might have learned something new."

The sheriff pushed open the front door and slipped out of the front seat.

Marcus exited the vehicle second and moved around to the back door to open it for Dakota. She'd long since grown accustomed to Agent Clement's insistence on manners towards women. A bit old school, but where she'd grown up, a little bit of chivalry was the least of her problems. In fact, though she'd never admit it to the bodybuilding BAU agent, she found it charming.

She nodded politely as she slipped from the vehicle and confronted the whir of red and blue reflecting off the dusty rest stop parking lot. Ahead, she watched where one of the deputies was now speaking to the sheriff in quick, hushed tones. The deputy was holding up his phone, and it looked as if he were showing an image to his supervisor.

Dakota stood by the car for a moment, the door behind her still open. Briefly, she felt an urge to turn, throw herself in the vehicle and lock the doors. She felt the comforting weight of the pain-relievers in her pocket. Was she ready for all of this? The lights, the police...

Her eyes moved towards the body beneath the tarp.

"Coroner hasn't come by yet?" she muttered, her curiosity quelling some of her fears.

Agent Clement followed her stare. "Some jurisdiction dispute," he whispered back.

She wanted to scowl but kept her expression calm. "So they just left the body to rot?"

Marcus gave a quick shake of his head. "Someone's going to lose a job over it, but not us. You good?"

"Peachy keen," she replied, her fingers grazing her turtleneck.

The two of them moved in tandem, striding towards the sheriff, the deputy, and the body behind them beneath the tarp.

Dakota kept her hands at her side, thumbs hooked in her pockets. She didn't like pocketing her entire hand—made it difficult to react.

As they neared the law enforcement officers, gravel crunching under foot, Agent Clement leaned his substantial frame towards Dakota and whispered, "Mind using that sixth sense of yours?"

She snorted. "It's not a sixth sense."

"Whatever you call it. Intuition, gut-instinct..."

"I watch people," she murmured back, "That's it."

"People-watching, right. Well..."

She paused briefly, a few paces away from the conversing law enforcement. One thing about training MMA—one had to react in a split second to even the most violent attack. Not just one, but multiple coming from all angles all in a matter of half a second. A single misstep, a single failure to react meant injury, knockout, or worse.

She'd always had a knack for studying her opponents. From the twitch of an eyelash to the flinch of a pinkie. From the way a muscle might bunch, or a body might lean, or an eye might glance. The same skills that had helped her "people-watch" as she called it also helped in other aspects.

The sheriff, for instance, was right-handed, judging by the placement of his holster. But he was standing on his off foot, his body directed *away* from the deputy, but his brow furrowed in concern, his ear inclined. A contradiction. The posture was one of a superior to a subordinate, bordering on disrespect. But the expression was one of extreme interest.

The conclusion was clear: the deputy's information pertaining to the case was more important to the sheriff than social standing in that moment.

The deputy was displaying his phone and muttering beneath his breath. Every so often, he glanced back over his shoulder towards the body.

"They found the victim," Dakota said after a moment, quietly. "Identified her. Lab isn't awake now—means they had a fingerprint match in a local database, readily accessible."

The sheriff paused, glancing back suddenly. "What was that?"

Dakota held up her hands. "Sorry. Nothing."

"Did you say...," the sheriff trailed off, looking confused.

Marcus looked smug.

Now, though, the officer with the military cut turned to face them. The same easy posture, the same inclination of his shoulders away from both. Small physical cues, but a wealth of information. Dakota wasn't a fan of disrespect, but Marcus couldn't care less.

Agent Clement said, "Well? Did you ID the victim?"

The sheriff was still frowning, shooting suspicious looks towards Dakota before clearing his throat and jutting a thumb towards the phone in his deputy's hand. "Afraid so," he said. "Twenty-five years old, Michayla Shirer. An afterschool instructor—that's how we have her prints." The sheriff jammed his hands into his pockets, glaring into the dark, his back directed towards the body.

Dakota frowned. "Was she reported missing?"

"Forty-eight hours ago," the sheriff replied.

"She's been missing for two days?"

"Yeah, looks like the theory holds. Our killer abducts his victims, holds them for a couple of days, then kills them."

"Only the two victims, though, yes?"

"That's right. First one was last week. Amber Reid, twenty-nine. She was found forty miles from here, also at a rest stop, also looking like she'd been dragged through a cheese grater." The sheriff pressed his lips in a thin, disapproving line. "Two so far by this so-called Motorcycle Murderer."

Dakota winced but hid her expression just as quickly.

"Do you think it's only one guy?" she asked.

The sheriff sighed, massaging the bridge of his nose. "Christ—we've considered multiple... Do you have insight on it?"

Dakota gave a quick shake of her head. "Bikers often move in gangs," she said simply. "If witnesses at the crime scenes heard a motorcycle fleeing the area, our best bet might be to rub elbows with those sorts."

"Biker gangs?"

"And the like."

The sheriff grunted. "Your lead is your lead. I'm still trying to get a damn coroner out here. But look, if you do go after bikers, just keep in mind these types will have criminal records. Dangerous in more ways than one. And I'm not just talking about our suspect. Some of them have quite literally gotten away with murder."

Dakota nodded at each word, and simply said, "Thank you. We'll be careful."

The deputy behind the sheriff cleared his throat, holding up a finger like a student in school. "Excuse me," he said, waving the same finger.

She looked towards the man, frowning. The sheriff seemed to have almost forgotten the fellow was there and turned with an irritated glance. "What?" he demanded.

"We might have a lead," the younger cop said, clearing his throat. "Michayla Shirer's family thinks they know who did this. They're at the station now and want to talk with someone." The deputy shifted his phone nervously in his hand, half extending it then retracting it.

"Christ," the sheriff muttered, "what time is it?"

Dakota was already glancing at her own phone. After 10:00 pm already. She glanced towards Marcus, content to let him make the decision.

The muscular man frowned, cleared his throat then said, "They might not be as open to share come morning. We can meet with them now. Can we borrow a driver?"

CHAPTER FOUR

Dakota sat in the back once more, staring through the windshield, over the arm of the deputy who'd been assigned to drive them to the station where Mr. and Mrs. Shirer were waiting. The vehicle moved at a more appropriate speed through the city streets, leaving the long, desolate road behind, the mountains fading in the rearview mirror.

Dakota glanced down at her phone, studying the images Agent Clement had sent, along with the updated, digital files on the case. Now that the second victim had been identified, she frowned at the driver's license photo of the young woman. Mid-twenties, smiling, a light dusting of freckles, Michayla Shirer hadn't deserved to die.

Dakota swiped the file to the first victim—the one from the previous week. Amber Reid, late twenties this time. Dark hair, olive skin, no freckles. She'd also gone missing two days before her body was found.

Dakota slowly lowered her phone, frowning at the likely options. The killer was abducting them first, taking his time with them... Torture? Sexual assault? This second theory might point to the possibility of gang violence. If multiple aggressors were involved, it might suggest a biker gang was using the victims for their own depraved pleasure before killing them and dumping them.

She lowered her phone, still frowning, trying not to think back to the last time she'd been examining a case file. Trying not to think about the way it had all ended.

Agent Clement sat in the front seat, but instead of watching the road, he was watching her, glancing in her direction with a raised eyebrow.

"What?" she said, pocketing her phone.

"Despondent?"

"Excuse me?"

"The word—have you heard it?"

Dakota frowned. "Yes, Marcus. I preferred your ice wizard."

He raised his hands in mock surrender. "You used to like my word puzzles."

"Yeah? Everyone knows despondent Marcus. Are you trying to make a point?" She shot a look towards the deputy who was doing his best to look like he wasn't listening.

"Should I be?" he said, his tone as even as ever.

"I'm fine, Clement. You're the one who wanted me here."

"Yes. And I still do. You're excellent at what you do, Dakota, even though you refuse to take credit. If I had half the instincts you did, I'd already be a station chief."

"Don't flatter me."

"I'm not. I'm complimenting you."

She crossed her arms and let out a faint sigh as Marcus turned back around to watch the road again. Ahead, Dakota spotted a large, government building, with long steps past metal barriers blocking the road.

Their deputy pulled towards a security check point, guiding them to a halt outside the police station.

Dakota's gaze flicked towards the large double doors at the top of the steps.

The Shirers were waiting in there. They claimed to have a lead.

Meeting a grieving family was never easy, but interviewing one in order to glean useful information? Nearly impossible unless an agent had their head on straight.

Dakota slipped a hand in her pocket as the security checkpoint opened, allowing them entrance into the parking lot.

***

Dakota settled at the interview table in the precinct's break room. Nevada cops had it good, or so it seemed. Two vending machines, an espresso-maker, and cushioned couches lining the wall. Now, though, Dakota felt the gravity of the situation. A clean-cut, well-dressed couple, as if they'd just come from church, though it wasn't Sunday, sat at the table. Both of them had red-ringed eyes, but now were presenting a united, stoic front, waiting for Marcus and Dakota to settle.

She admired this courage in the face of grief. Dakota preferred keeping her own emotions to herself as well.

Agent Clement spoke first, clearing his throat, and reaching a large, comforting hand across the table, patting the back of the chair where Mrs. Shirer sat stiff and straight-backed.

"Thank you for coming in on such a difficult night," Marcus said in that soothing tone of his. He'd always had a bedside manner.

Dakota, for her part, watched their postures. Read their body language. Leaning in towards one another. A close marriage then? The red-ringed eyes suggested grief. The stoic nature now confronted by law enforcement, coupled with the fancy outfits suggested a fondness for appearances. A grieving, upper-class couple. Dakota felt a pang of sorrow for the Shirers but kept her emotions in check.

"Thank you... Mr.," the husband began, trailing off to allow Marcus to fill in the blank.

"Agent Clement," Marcus provided with a quick nod and a smile.

"Yes. Agent Clement. Thank you. My brother works here," Mr. Shirer said, his lips barely moving as he exhaled between words. He seemed on the verge of a panic attack but managed to keep himself together. "He informed me when my daughter's name...," he swallowed now. "We... we already assumed the worst. She was supposed to meet us yesterday. When she didn't show..." He trailed off, biting back a sob.

His wife was gripping his arm as if it were a mooring post, keeping her in harbor. Mrs. Shirer said, "Michayla was a free spirit." The woman had a pleasant, steady voice, despite her expression. "She... she hitchhiked and didn't live at home. We don't even know if she had a bed to sleep on."

Marcus shot Dakota a quick glance and then looked back towards the parents. "I'm very sorry for your loss. You said she was going to meet with you yesterday?"

"Yes," Mrs. Shirer said, sobbing but biting off the sound. She went silent for a moment, and the others allowed her this concession, waiting as she gathered herself. Then, exhaling briefly, she continued, "we were going to patch things up. We... we were going to be a family again. She said she was sorry about how she left. I—I made her favorite peach cobbler. Cleaned the house."

"Twice," her husband murmured. He smiled faintly, but then the expression died.

Mrs. Shirer nodded but hid her face again, her shoulders trembling.

Dakota felt tears threatening her own eyes. This was the part of the job she'd never gotten used to. Never would. She'd been the one to tell the parents of the killer's last victim during the case three months ago. She'd insisted she be the one to tell them.

They hadn't been nearly so composed. They'd broken down, weeping, and blaming the cops, the FBI—blaming Dakota.

And she'd agreed with them. It was why she'd left. But now, sitting here, facing similar pain, she felt her hands go cold. A sweat prickling her fingers.

Would she make the same mistakes as last time? Would she be able to focus?

Clearing her throat roughly, she said, her voice husky from lack of use, “It was mentioned you had a lead. You know who did this to your daughter?”

It was like watching a transformation. Both the Shirer's faces morphed into masks of rage. Eyes flashed, lips pressed, jaws grit.

“Yes!” Mr. Shirer snapped, pointing a finger across the table. An accusing finger, not quite aimed at anyone in the room, but aimed, nonetheless. “That bastard boyfriend of hers!” Mrs. Shirer gripped her husband's arm even tighter.

He continued, “We told her he was bad news. Told her to steer clear of the no-good lowlife scumbag. But of course, that only pushed her further into his disgusting arms.”

“Who is this boyfriend?” Dakota said, her tone dispassionate, trying to keep things professional, not just for her sake, but for theirs.

Mr. Shirer exhaled shakily but calmed a bit. He nodded briefly. “I—we—well....” he winced, glancing at his wife.

“We never met the guy,” Mrs. Shirer interjected, also flinching. “She wouldn't let us. Didn't give us a name. But she told us he was part of a biker gang. She said he was a free spirit like she was...” Mrs. Shirer's nose wrinkled in disgust. “If I ever hear the phrase *free spirit* used to justify irresponsible life choices again, I think I'll puke.”

Now, her husband's arm was clasping hers. The two of them remained straight-backed in their neat, Sunday school clothing. They watched the agents without blinking.

“Do you have a description of the boyfriend?” Marcus asked gently.

“Saw a picture on her phone once,” Mrs. Shirer said. “I wasn't snooping!” she added hastily. “Just saw it. He... he was Hispanic, short but muscular. Lots of tattoos.” She looked disgusted again.

Dakota tugged at her sleeves, making sure none of her own ink was visible.

“And the name of his biker gang,” Dakota asked. “Know it?”

“Yes,” both parents said simultaneously.

Mr. Shirer said, “She got a bumper sticker on that little scooter she drove around—before it broke.”

“Devil's Renegades,” Mrs. Shirer said simply, her lip still curled. “They're local. They're bad news. And they're the ones who murdered my baby!” Her voice ended in a high-pitched warble, turning to another sob.

Dakota let loose a shaky sigh, glancing at Marcus now, who took another moment to try and console the grieving parents. Not that it was any use—nothing they said or did would change the pain.

But... they could prevent another family from going through this. They could bring justice.

Dakota pushed back from the table suddenly, nodding stiffly to each parent in turn. “Washroom,” she said quickly, hand darting to her pocket.

“I'll meet you out front,” Marcus said, looking at her.

She frowned. “Umm... you want to check these guys out tonight?”

Marcus snorted. “They're bikers. They don't have a bedtime.”

Dakota shrugged, and hooked her thumbs into her pockets, trying to hide the trembling as she hurried away from the table, pressed out into the long hall, and hotfooted in the direction of the bathroom. She needed a bump. Just a little something to take the edge off.

Then, after some chemical help, they'd go and confront a biker gang in search of a free-spirit ex-boyfriend. Murderer, though? The sheriff's warnings also came echoing back. Danger. That's what he'd said to expect with gangs like this. Criminals, violent men and murderers.

The only question: Were the Devil's Renegades responsible for *these* murders?

CHAPTER FIVE

Night came quick and darkness fell across the horizon. Dakota glanced towards the digital clock on their rental vehicle. 11:59. She stared, counting the seconds, and then the clock hit midnight. She straightened, peering through the windshield as gravel crunched beneath the tires. Marcus guided them into an alley behind the bar.

"You sure this is a good idea?" Dakota muttered, glancing towards her clean-cut partner. The enormous, body-building agent flashed a schoolboy smile and a wink.

"You saw the bikes out front. They're still here." He wrinkled his nose, going quiet and holding a meaty hand to his ear. "Hear that? Horrible taste in music."

Indeed, a loud, pumping, blaring mixture of rock and heavy metal blasted from the small, seedy desert dive bar.

An auto shop and an abandoned gas station helped form the alley, which was littered with refuse, old furniture and what looked like a body bag, but—on closer inspection—proved to be the discarded cushions of an old sofa. The cushions were stained with something red.

Dakota frowned, craning her neck to catch the large sign on the edge of the road.

Nowhere. The sign read. *Bar and Grill.*

The rows of motorcycles beneath the sign were arranged like tin soldiers, in neat, clean, polished rows.

Dakota frowned towards the vehicles, wondering if one of these things had been used to drag the two women to their deaths. She could imagine some greasy, bearded dude with neck tattoos chaining the helpless women to the back of a bike, only after using them for perverse pleasures.

Would they find the ex-boyfriend here? Was he really involved?

Dakota blinked a few times, trying to quiet her racing thoughts. She wanted to stay sharp—to focus.

But this was difficult to do, especially with something like existential dread constantly nipping at her heels.

Marcus was scanning his phone, studying the report from Major Crimes. "Devil's Renegades," Agent Clement murmured. "This is their favorite spot. You good to go?”

Dakota hesitated, but then nodded quickly. Instead of meeting her partner's gaze, she pushed open the door and slipped into the alley.

Immediately, she was confronted by the odor of refuse and urine. She also detected the faintest undertones of vomit.

Charming.

She rolled up her sleeves now, hooking her thumbs into her pockets and strolling around the side of the building towards the front entrance. The second door slammed behind her, and the heavy footfalls of Marcus Clement came in pursuit.

As she strolled, her sleeves rolled back, she felt the cool wind against her normally covered arms. She also glanced down to note the sleeve tattoo on her left forearm of a dove being eaten by a snake. That one had been the idea of an ex-boyfriend of hers. The small cartoon mouse on her right arm had all been her idea. And the big skull and crossbones, like from a pirate's flag, just inside the wrist, had been a complete mistake. She still couldn't remember getting it.

Most of her tattoos were of a bygone area. She had them up her arms, along her torso, and on her back. While fighting, most of the athletes had been covered in the things.

As an FBI agent, though, it didn't exactly *scream* promotion to walk into a quarterly review with arms looking like the denizens of *Nowhere.*

Marcus caught up with her as she reached the front door of the bar. Elbow first, she pushed her way through the dingy, smudged glass.

She swallowed faintly and could feel Marcus tensing at her side. She shot him a look and he gave her a significant glance, raising a quick eyebrow.

She flashed a thumbs up, and turned back to examine the patrons of *Nowhere.* This seedy joint, in the middle of nowhere was still active well into the night. Rough sorts with leathers and facial hair—even on some of the women—lounged around stools or near billiards tables. Drinks clinked against marble counters or circular metal tables. Raucous laughter competed with the blaring music for dominance.

As Dakota scanned the dozen or so patrons, her eyes slipped behind the counter—no bartender visible. She wondered if they'd retired for the evening or, perhaps, if one of the billiards players or patrons was also the proprietor.

She noticed something else.

Most of the bikers were white or Hispanic. Agent Clement shifted uncomfortably next to her, also surveying the space. A few of the patrons were glancing in their direction now, mad dogging. Dakota met their glares or askance glances with even looks of her own. She'd grown up a fighter but had always been a professional.

One fellow, in a crummy bandanna, pulled the object back and wiped at a glaze of sweat on his brow. He pushed back from the table and jerked his head towards the agents. Two other patrons looked up as well, their eyes hooded, their expression bleary.

"What do you want?" the man in the bandanna called out suddenly.

Dakota felt out of place in her neat outfit standing next to a linebacker in a suit. The two of them met the derisive shout with polite expressions.

"We were hoping to ask a few questions," Dakota said, her eyes moving from one face to the next, catching glares wreathed in shadow and smoke.

The pungent scent of cigarettes, and the sweeter odor of weed, lingered openly on the air. A woman and a younger man at the counter had a bong between them, making no effort to conceal it.

"You cops?" the man in the bandanna demanded, hitching up his jeans and displaying an overhanging beer belly.

Marcus flashed a disarming smile, keeping his tone friendly despite the tenor of the biker bar. "FBI," he said. "Like my partner said, just want to ask a few questions."

Another biker stood up suddenly. His chair screeched as it scraped against the ground, sliding back. This fellow sauntered over, his shoulders the size of bowling balls. He was shorter than Marcus by a good foot but made up for it in attitude. He had silver-speckled hair, receding at the temples and a sneer that hinted at a repressed midlife crisis.

"You a big one, ain't you?" this newcomer asked, jutting his chin towards Clement. "And you'd be double purty if not for them stains," he added, wiggling his eyebrows to Dakota and glancing down towards her tattoos. It took her a moment to realize she was being insulted, albeit hypocritically—especially given the man's own neck tattoo in the shape of a noose. She felt a sharp sting at his words—appearances mattered. She didn't like having hers mocked.

"Does anyone know a woman by the name of Michayla Shirer?" Marcus called out, projecting his voice. The couple by the bar with the bong winced, ducking their heads as if against a headache. A few of the other patrons grumbled, nursing their drinks.

A third biker, who'd been playing billiards, slowly approached, gripping his pool cue by the thin end, holding it like a cudgel.

Dakota glanced at their postures. Poised. Knuckles tight. Shoulders set. Eyes flared. Aggression imminent. It all cataloged in a split-second, her mind making the connection and suddenly warning her with a prickle down her spine and a sudden flood of adrenaline.

Still, she knew how to mask her own emotions. Her hands remained steady, loose at her sides, her eyes remained attentive, engaged with the surrounding men.

She patted Marcus on the small of his back, nudging him in warning.

He gave her a quick look and a nod. But held up a single finger as if to say, *one more chance.*

He tried a final time. "We're here about a murder," he said. "Michayla Shirer. She was only twenty-five. Please. Do any of you have any—"

"Why your lady got that buggy ear?" A voice suddenly called from the back of the room. "Look at her ear—looks like a big ol' pimple. Pop it for me, big man! Pop the bitch's ear!"

A few voices laughed in the smoke-infused room. Dakota's eyes narrowed.

The man with the pool cue chuckled, pointing a finger at Marcus. "He's not wrong," the fellow said in a slow, slurring voice. "Hell, bet she'd blend right in this late at night with all them tattoos if we took ya outside. Wanna try it?" He flashed a gap-toothed grin and basked in the chuckles and giggles of some of the surrounding hooligans.

The couple at the bar looked disconcerted by the direction of the conversation, and, on tottering footsteps, moved further down the seats, away from the three men facing the two agents.

Dakota, for her part, was examining—calm and cool as she could manage—the speaker's throat. A quick knuckle to the larynx and he wouldn't make jokes like that.

She could feel time slowing, or, perhaps, her own thoughts speeding. She even tilted her head in frank curiosity. The man must have been really drunk to think that sort of humor would go over well with her.

Marcus, as always, attempting to keep the peace, brushed the comment off with a sniff and a quick shake of his head. He reached out towards Dakota as if to hold her at bay.

She hadn't given any indication of aggression. Not yet. But Marcus knew her well. He always had. This had always been one of Dakota's greatest assets when in the cage. But, also, in law-enforcement. Her ability to keep her emotions, her physical reactions camouflaged always gave her the advantage of surprise.

People never expected the sudden, unforgiving, brutal violence to erupt from a woman of average-height, average-size and, in their minds, docile bearing. But as a woman, the best way she'd found to compensate for a size disadvantage was to avoid slow escalation. Rather, an unexpected, brutally violent first strike never gave the opponent a chance to even react. Her femininity, her training under Casper, had taught her one thing: punch hard enough and the problem ends on the first strike. Too soft and things got messy.

She could feel the adrenaline surging. Could feel her own emotions rising. The man with the pool cue was poking at Marcus now. Muttering, "Think that'll come off in the wash, huh?"

Dakota tensed, hand curled. Marcus glanced over and his eyes widened. "No—hang on, Steele. It's fine. Let it go!"

The three bikers standing nearest all chuckled. Their attention turning from Agent Clement to Dakota. "What, this bitty thing?" one of them said. "I'd like to go a couple rounds with her. Whadaya say, doll? I got a trailer out back." The one with the beer gut wiggled his eyebrows and reached out to stroke her cheek.

Dakota said, simply, "Stop."

She didn't like violence. Wouldn't force it, but sometimes the inevitable came.

He poked her again. "I said stop," she repeated, calm, quiet.

He stared at her now, sneering. "You drowsy, girl? I'm speaking to you!" He poked her again. Again. He suddenly leaned in with a smirk, his lips puckering.

Dakota caught a glimpse of Marcus's face in that moment. The moment the man's lips neared her own, Clement winced. His gaze carried a faint resignation to the inevitable.

He couldn't be too mad, she reasoned. She had asked the man to stop. She moved her face; the man's lips grazed her cheek.

Then all hell broke loose, and Dakota carried the key.

CHAPTER SIX

One moment, everything had been in stasis, calm, poised. The three men had thought they'd been picking on a couple of softies in suits. No small amount of alcohol or poor late-night decisions had led to this moment. The racist comments were one thing. The refusal to help a murder investigation another.

But touching her? Kissing?

That was a no-no.

Dakota barely even processed her reaction. It was pure instinct.

The man who'd insulted Marcus caught her fist first—knuckles to the neck, just like she'd been considering.

She punched *through,* feet under shoulders, turning at the waist, knee forward. A motion she must have practiced a thousand times. Aiming for the vulnerable throat, full force. A sudden wave of anger surged through her as her fist connected. Flesh to skin. Knuckles deep.

The man let out a croaking sound like a drowning frog, his eyes bugging. His own hands darted to his neck as he reeled back, stumbled over a chair then hit the ground with a weak, whimpering moan.

For a moment, everything seemed to go still.

Dakota blinked in surprise at the effectiveness of the blow. She often still shadow-boxed to maintain cardio, but it had been a while since she'd actually had to put someone down.

A few of the other bikers in the bar cursed sharply, rising to their feet. Marcus grimaced, muttering beneath his breath, "Shoulda let it go."

Dakota muttered back. "He touched me."

Marcus sighed.

Now, the man with the bandanna and the beer-gut stared between them, gaping. Just as quickly though, his eyes narrowed into a mean, piggy little scowl. Courage came in the form of three other men, now pushing through the tables. One of them sent a metal stool clattering to the floor in his urgency.

"Bitch," beer-gut said. "That's my cousin!"

"He'll be fine," Dakota murmured, once again masking her emotions. She stood straight-backed, quiet, calm. No sign of aggression, no indication of the adrenaline now pulsing through her body.

As a fighter, she knew the value of self-control. At least, as much of it as she could manage. She'd made her point. No need to escalate.

Unless...

Two of the men suddenly darted in. One of them bellowed, "Pigs! Get out!"

Dakota heard something scrape behind her and whirled in time to dodge a chair flung at her head from a woman with a face tattoo.

"Marcus!" she shouted in warning.

Agent Clement held his hands out in placating protest. "Please—let's just all calm down—"

But too late.

Now, five of the patrons converged at once. Two of them went for Marcus. A third hung back, checking on the fallen man with the pool cue. Two more tried to tackle Dakota.

But she was moving. Cage-fighting trained for one-on-one combat. Multiple assailants weren't her area of expertise. But at the same time, she could deal with one at a time.

She rolled back over one of the tables, sending a beer bottle smashing to the ground. Her feet hit the floor and she turned sharply to catch the blow of the woman with the face tattoo. By placing the table behind her, she bought herself seconds. Beer-gut was charging from the other direction, but now tangled in the stools.

Dakota took the opportunity. Voice even, breathing in shallow huffs she muttered to the woman. "Stay back—let this go."

For a moment, something like fear flashed in her assailant's gaze, but just as quickly the look vanished and the woman let out a feral screech like a bobcat. She lunged.

Dakota caught the blow on her forearms. She ducked her head, shoulders low, absorbing a sudden onslaught of slaps and punches. None of them made much progress. Inexperienced fighters often gassed themselves in the first few moments of combat.

This, it seemed, was no exception.

Once she'd weathered the initial blows, still rotating to keep the table between her and beer-gut, Dakota then loosed a shot of her own.

To the kidney. Then a second to the chest.

Face-tattoo stumbled back with a gasping grunt, hitting the counter and sending a couple of glasses clattering behind the barricade.

Good thing too—beer-gut had now reached her. He came in with an overhand right. She leaned away from the blow, but he lowered his head in the same motion, driving it into her face. Skull met lip. Pain blossomed in her mouth. She stumbled back.

He was taller, larger, and smellier than Dakota. Which meant this time she didn't want to let him in close. A grappling match, especially with a large person in a multiple-assailant situation would prove difficult to manage.

So she lurched back, then kicked out with her front foot. A straight shove-kick to the breadbasket. The man doubled over, wheezing and gasping.

All of it had taken less than five seconds, but to Dakota everything was action and reaction. Tensed muscles, furrowed brows, shifting feet, the sudden pause, the surge of rage, the moment of indecision followed subsequently by rapid and violent action. All of it made sense.

For the first time in weeks, she flashed a genuine smile, reaching up and wiping the blood from the corner of her bruised lip. She'd missed this. Missed the movement, the motion, the danger, the exertion.

She didn't have time to enjoy herself too much, though.

Marcus was in trouble too.

As she spun on her heel, yanking her foot out of the grasping reach of Face-tattoo, she spotted her six-foot-six, three-hundred-pound, bodybuilding gentle giant of a companion. He was scooting back on his heels, hands deftly blocking attacks, occasionally gripping a fist to soften the blow but then letting it go.

"Come on guys," Clement was saying, "cut it out. This is pointless!"

His tone carried the tenor of a doting schoolteacher trying to wrangle unruly children. But he hadn't spotted the knife. One of the bikers by the bar was approaching from behind, a snarl curling his lip, a switchblade sprouting from one hand.

Ten feet away. Five.

Dakota was too far to intervene.

The knife flashed.

Dakota lurched, using the momentum to grab the closest object at hand.

A beer bottle. She launched it with a shout, sending the thing end over end. It struck the knife-wielding biker in the chest.

He jolted in surprise, hesitating briefly.

This was all the time Dakota needed to cover the distance in three lurching steps before bringing a strong left shin into his gut. The man, though, was made of sterner stuff than his companions. He maintained his feet and tried to slash at her.

"HEY!" Marcus suddenly bellowed, noticing the weapon now. His voicc boomed like a subwoofer, and his eyes suddenly blazed. "Don't you *dare*!" he yelled.

A meaty fist the size of a boxing glove pile-drove into the knife-wielder's chin. Suddenly the man went perpendicular with the floor, his head snapping back, his feet flying up.

Dakota grinned, whirling on her feet, hands up, ready for the next round. But Agent Clement, playing the adult for the moment, raised his hand, flashing a badge, his other gripping his firearm.

"FBI! Stop right now!"

A brief pause fell over the group. They'd already known they were assaulting feds, but now, at the sign of the giant with his hand on his equally large weapon, everyone went still. Dakota heard the faintest, satisfying *snap* of the holster.

Faint moans could be heard echoing in the room. Figures rolled on the ground, groaning at the beer-stained floors. Someone had shut the music off. The lingering aura of cigarette smoke now wafted in the quiet, and Dakota's eyes darted about, cataloging motions, paying attention to body language.

For the moment, it seemed, the fight had fled the Devil's Renegades.

Dakota's eyes landed on the woman she'd knocked down first. The face tattoo was slick with sweat, but also stippled with droplets of blood from a clearly busted nose. The woman was groaning, massaging her head with trembling fingers.

As Dakota stared and Marcus tried to retain order, she felt a gnawing sense of guilt suddenly form like a weight in her gut. The flecks of blood, the groan of pain, the woman on the ground, curled like a child tucked in bed.

She shivered. Memories came back.

And like that, the sense of exhilaration, of excitement, the cheap thrill of violence she'd once grown so accustomed to... vanished.

The bleak dark that had been her closest companion for decades and even more in the last few months came flooding back. It almost seemed to drain the world of color, drained the ground of stability. Her legs threatened to give out from under her.

Dakota could feel the effects of the pain killers alleviating now. She let out a shuddering gasp and suddenly dropped to her knees at the woman's side. "I'm sorry!" she said earnestly. "I'm sorry—so sorry! Are you okay?" her voice tremored. To her shame, Dakota felt tears suddenly form in her eyes as she knelt on the barroom floor, staring down at the woman she'd assaulted. Such a rarity for her—tears. And yet her they came at the oddest moment, her emotions erratic.

The woman with the face tattoo flinched, trying to jerk back. "Get off me, bitch!" she groaned.

"Sorry," Dakota said, reflexively. The tears traced inside her cheek now. Completely unbidden—tears that had no place in *Nowhere.* But the emotions threatened to consume her all the same. "Sorry," she murmured, her voice in a ghost of a whisper.

She was staring at the woman but seeing... *other* things. A still, small body. A failed choice. She should've listened to Marcus. Should've followed *his* lead.

"Agent Steele," a voice was saying from behind her. "Dakota?" gentle, but firm.

She blinked, still kneeling by the woman. One of her hands hovered in an attempt to try and console the injured woman, but at the same time, her spine prickled and she looked back.

Tears staining her cheeks, she realized everyone in the bar was watching her. Marcus studied her expression, his brow flickering in a frown for only a split-second, but then the usual warmth returned to his eyes. His hand was still on his holster though, and his intimidating shoulders were braced against the ogling of the bar's occupants.

"Enough," he said, firmly, pointing at the rest of them. "I'm in my right to drag every one of you off to prison. Do you know the sentence for attacking a federal officer?"

"Don't!" Dakota said suddenly, looking over. "It's fine," she said. *I started it,* she thought to herself with another burst of guilt.

She glanced back to the woman on the ground, reaching up with a trembling finger to wipe her tears away, then, in as muted a voice as she could manage, she whispered. "Do you know anything about Michayla Shirer?"

The injured woman had propped up on an elbow now, nursing her injured nose. She shot a suspicious look towards Dakota then to Marcus. A few of the men were grumbling. Beer-gut glared towards the woman. "Don't say shit, Becks."

"Ah sherrup, Jack," she returned. She pointed a finger towards Marcus. "Don't press no charges, an' I'll tell you what you wanna know."

Dakota pushed slowly to her feet, dusting at her knees. Marcus kept his hand on his holstered weapon but made a vague motion with one hand as if to say *go on.*

"Need you to say it," she said. But then Becks paused and shook her head. "Actually, nah—*you* say it," she pointed towards Dakota. "Weird bitch got a screw loose, but she ain't got liar's eyes."

Dakota blinked at this characterization. Then, swallowing her emotion as she was so often inclined to do, she said in an even tone, "We won't press charges if you can tell us anything about Michayla."

The woman snorted, looking Dakota in the eye. "You're telling the truth. I can tell. Right, well—"

"Shut up Becks!"

"Stuff it, Jack. No, look here. Little Michayla didn't belong here. She was moonlighting, you see."

Dakota shared a look with Marcus. "So you did see her?" Agent Clement asked across the bar.

A few of the other patrons had now returned to their conversations, their drinks, their darts, as if a little bit of impromptu violence was all par for the course for this particular establishment.

"Yeah, I seen her," said Becks. She now regained her feet, wobbling somewhat. When Dakota reached out to help her, the woman slapped the hand away. "Get off," she snapped. "I aint gonna screw you. Look, Michayla liked the guys. Liked the music. Liked the drugs. Liked the rides. That's it. She shouldn't have been here. And if you're saying she got got, I'm not surprised."

"Who was her boyfriend?" Dakota asked, her voice calm.

"Becks!" Jack growled.

Becks ignored him again. "No charges, right," she said pointedly.

"Right," Dakota insisted.

"Fair," Becks sighed. "No-good deadbeat, meth chef. Named Berno."

"And where might we find Berno?" said Dakota. "Does he have a last name? An address?"

The female biker just groaned, muttering as rivulets of blood streamed down her lip and gathered in the curve of a downturned grimace. "Address? No. Bit of a—"

"Free spirit?" Dakota guessed.

"I was gonna say asshole." She glared. "Berno just goes by Berno. Don't got a last name. I don't know where he lives, but I know where he'll be." Now Becks ignored the frowns around the room, and the low growl coming from the man with the freshly bruised belly. "He works at the gas station down the road. Morning shift. It's his uncle's place—

that old fart's a rough customer. One of the good ones." She winked.

Dakota wasn't sure quite how to interpret this endorsement from a woman who'd just attacked her with a folding chair. Still, she tried to stay on task. "The gas station five miles back?"

"That's the one. Big floppy advertising inflatable thing out front. Berno works the counter. Might let you bum a cig if you ask nicely." She pursed her lips and mimed something with her hand that Dakota didn't spend much time attempting to interpret.

She shot a look at Agent Clement and jerked her head towards the door. The big man frowned briefly, glancing towards the groaning men on the ground. But then he sighed, buttoned his holster and, backing away slowly, moved with Dakota back towards the door.

Again, the cloying, dark weight had settled on her shoulders once more. She wanted to cry, to curl up in her bed and shut off the lights. She wanted to be left alone, but at the same time the thing she dreaded most was to be left alone.

She noticed her hands tremoring now—a fighter's hands, but she wasn't sure how much longer she could put up a fight.

As she reached the exit, watched by the patrons in *Nowhere,* she murmured beneath her breath. "Should we check this gas station out?"

Marcus pushed through the door and waited for it to shut behind them before exhaling briefly into the night and answering. "It's getting late. Might need some sleep."

Dakota pictured the image of trying to rest in a strange place, in the dark. No—no far better to keep moving. She said, "Only a few hours until he's supposed to show up. I don't want anyone in there warning him off."

"Well... how about a compromise?" Marcus said, patting his pocket which jingled with keys.

Dakota paused but then groaned. "New Jersey?"

"New Jersey," he said with a grin and a nod. "Come on—it wasn't *so* bad. Just a few hours."

"You snore," she muttered, turning to move around the side of the building. Partly, because she wanted to lodge her protest, but partly too, because she didn't want to meet his gaze. She could feel him watching her. Feel the pity in his eyes.

Had he seen her crying? Was he, even now, regretting his decision to ask her to come back?

She let out a shaking little breath. As she moved towards the alley, taking the sidewalk in careful steps interjected by the odd glance back towards the front door to the bar to make sure it stayed shut, she expected a comment or a cleared throat.

But Marcus didn't say anything. After a moment, she heard his footsteps following after her. A long stride and a shorter one. Easygoing, careful motions compared to Dakota's quick, calculated steps. They made a good team.

She shot a look back at last and conjured a faint smile. "You still have that left hook."

He snorted. "You still go for the kidney."

"Ah well, you know. Habits."

He gave a good-natured laugh. The smile creasing his features came from somewhere deeper in a person's soul than Dakota knew how to access. She stared in some envy at the smile, but at the same time felt a flash of gratitude at least her partner could find happiness. Even while walking away from the hurled insults and fists behind them.

He shot another look over his shoulder, rubbed his jaw, then shrugged and reached the front of their loaner.

"New Jersey," he reminded her.

"Right, right," she said, slipping into the backseat now.

A bit of shut-eye—uncomfortable as it was bound to be, the same as the last stake-out they'd had in Jersey—and then they'd confront a potential killer.

The Shirers had seemed confident Michayla's new boyfriend had been involved in her death. Would he cave on questioning? Would he even be at his place of employment so soon after?

Dakota frowned as Marcus pulled out of the alley and angled back towards the long, dusty road outside the lonely watering hole.

CHAPTER SEVEN

Marcus Clement refused to admit he snored. But just in case, he'd attached one of his night-bag breathe-right strips before drifting off, and now, a few hours of poor sleep later, he blinked blearily in the front seat of their borrowed vehicle.

As his vision adjusted, he peered out at the small gas station they'd parked in front of. No other vehicles in the lot just yet. But that didn't mean their overnight stake-out would be for nothing.

Still, it had left him with a crick in his neck. He massaged at the top of his spine, groaning as he did, but trying to keep the sounds to a minimum. At least in New Jersey, when the two partners had been forced to sleep in a car together, they'd had working vents. The chill, open-space Nevada night had been uncomfortable to say the least.

He stretched as best he could, his large forearms bumping the steering wheel. The gas station ahead, complete with grimy windows and old-fashioned do-it-yourself pumps didn't seem like the stomping grounds of a serial killer.

But in his twenty years of experience, Agent Clement had seen all sorts act out their depravity on the world.

He tried not to think about it too much. The more he dwelled on that sort of thing, the harder it was to stay sane.

At the thought, he glanced in the mirror, frowning towards where Agent Steele slept in the back.

She looked almost peaceful with her head reclining against the window. She had one cauliflower ear from her old fighting career and preferred to wear her hair neat and cut shoulder-length. All of it perfectly uniform, like a longer bowl cut. She was still passably attractive save a faint scar along the underside of her cheek which had never properly healed. Another gift from her combat past.

Normally, she didn't sleep so soundly.

He sighed as he stared in the mirror, watching his partner.

He hadn't been lying to her. He trusted her. Needed her on this case. Things back at the office were... tense. He was up for a promotion, but it was starting to look like he'd be passed over again. Marcus had never been cutthroat enough to play office politics.

Besides, did he really want to sit behind some desk somewhere?

No... No, he belonged in the field, sleeping in cars outside dusty gas stations.

It wasn't just for her help as an investigator that he'd approached her.

But also...

He swallowed faintly, closing his eyes against the first few glimmers of sunlight over the distant mountains.

He blamed himself. He shouldn't have been so hard on her when she'd failed to follow his lead. He'd known they were going after the wrong guy. He'd insisted, but she'd ignored him. Her own history—the disappearance of her baby sister, decades ago, had clouded her judgment.

And so three months ago... another girl had died. The similarities between this recent case and the one from Dakota's childhood had become clearer *after* the fact. Some psycho targeting little girls. He should've said something. He knew that now. Should've asked Dakota to take a step back.

He thought he'd been doing the right thing. Thought he'd been helping her get past it.

But in the end, a girl had died.

Dakota had followed a bad lead, had ignored Marcus, and now hated herself for it.

He hadn't helped. He could still remember the fire in his voice after they'd found the new body. *I told you!* He'd bellowed. *I told you!*

He'd caught himself quickly. Left the room before he said anything he'd truly regretted. Now... now he wished he could've taken those words back. Wished he could've just hugged Dakota and been there for her.

Maybe she wouldn't have handed in her badge and gun then. Maybe she wouldn't be so...

Broken.

He looked in the mirror again and felt his heart twist.

If anyone deserved a good turn, it was Agent Steele. Part of the reason he loved working with her was because he knew he could count on her. She was trustworthy in nearly every aspect of the job. She never participated in gossip. Made others stop if she was around just by her presence. She didn't lie, either. She went out of her way to tell the truth.

Plus... as evident from a few hours ago, she kicked ass. And often felt bad about it after.

He smiled fondly, staring at the mirror, other, better memories replacing the more recent ones. They'd been partners for nearly a decade now. The last three months hadn't felt right without her.

Still... Dakota Steele came with demons. Not just the ones she'd picked up three months ago, while hunting a killer who slipped away.

No—she carried things that went back decades. Marcus wasn't the sort to root around in people's personal life, and employee files were sealed. But Dakota had been the one to tell him, two years into their partnership about her sister's disappearance more than twenty years ago.

Some wounds didn't heal properly.

Never would on this side of eternity.

Marcus breathed a long huff of air, blinking in the rising glimmer of light over the craggy mountains.

Just then, he heard the grumble of an approaching engine. He perked up, sitting straight-backed in the cushioned chair. He reached up, peeling the breathe-right nasal strip and placing it in the small, collapsible, pocket can for trash Dakota had gotten him years ago.

That woman didn't just have a neat bone, she had an entire skeleton. The only times he ever really saw her cranky—or expressing any emotion really—was when she was fighting or when someone made a mess. Especially a mess she had to live with. He shivered at a memory of that very same trip to New Jersey. The omelet debacle had nearly ended their partnership right there.

Once he'd made sure the car was tidy enough, he cleared his throat, reached back, and tapped his partner's knee.

"Dakota," he whispered. "I think that's our guy." She twisted a bit, but continued sleeping, her eyes sealed.

He frowned, tapping harder now and turning to extend his reach and direct his voice. "Agent Steele!" he said. "We have company!"

She continued to slumber. The aftereffects of one too many beers like the ones he'd smelled on her back at her apartment?

He winced at the thought and tried again. "Dakota!"

Her eyes snapped open, and her hands tensed. It took her a few moments to reorient, blinking in the shadowed passenger seat. Once she spotted Marcus, her fists uncurled—she opened her mouth to speak, but then closed it slowly, studying his expression.

Dakota had always had a knack for reading people, reading situations. And now, only seconds after having woken, she realized something was afoot.

Marcus jutted a finger through the windshield towards a man on a cheap, rusted motorbike puttering into the gas station.

The fellow in question wore a visored helmet that obscured his features. He had a no-sleeve cut-off t-shirt and ratty jeans. A thick necklace of beads draped down to his chest, dangling past a cartoon skeleton with a snake for a tongue.

Marcus shot Dakota one last look and then began to move. He pushed open the door and began slipping out into the early morning. "Berno?" he called, his voice projecting. "I'd like to—"

He didn't get a chance to finish. The man on the bike spun around, yanking something from his hip. A flash of metal. Dakota shouted a warning from the back seat. But Agent Clement was already moving, flinging himself to the side, large hands over his head.

Then came the gunshots. The side window of their vehicle shattered first. Glass rained down like hailstones. Agent Clement was already bent double, draping over the dash, towards the passenger seat, his fingers scrambling for his own weapon.

A second passed and then he heard the sound of a roaring engine.

"Go! Go!" Dakota shouted. "He's getting away!"

Marcus jolted upright once more. He shot a look in the rearview mirror where Agent Steele was fully awake now, perked, her window down, her own weapon in her left hand—she could shoot just as well with either.

Marcus twisted the keys, put the vehicle in gear and floored it.

They kicked up dust and smoke as they tore out of the parking lot, speeding after the fleeing biker. The vehicle jolted as they jumped a curb then tore onto the lonely highway.

The biker sped out ahead, tearing down the asphalt path, through the lonely flatlands, deeper into the desert. Agent Clement gripped his steering wheel, glaring through the windshield. The window to his left had been shattered and as they picked up speed, cool, desert wind ripped through the confines of the vehicle. "You calling for backup?" Marcus shouted over his shoulder.

"Twenty minutes away!" Dakota retorted from the back seat.

"Great," he growled beneath his breath, picking up speed. "Darn it. Dang it!" His frustration mounted as they closed the distance between their bumper and the fleeing crotch rocket.

The biker's weapon—small-caliber judging by the window damage—was now out of sight as his whole focus was directed towards fleeing. Agent Clement floored the gas pedal, trying to draw closer to the biker. They were gaining, their engine outpacing the smaller vehicle.

"He's going to brake!" Dakota shouted suddenly. "Clement, slow down!"

"Almost got him!" Marcus shouted back, hands on the wheel, trying to nudge against the back tire of the fleeing motorbike.

"Marcus, slow down!"

"I've almost got him!"

Only a few feet of asphalt separated the bumper of their loaner and the back tire of Berno's motorbike. Three feet. Two... inches. The vehicles sped on the lonely highway beneath the sunrise.

"Marcus!"

"Almost there..."

Clement's hands tensed, his eyes narrowed, he winced, bracing for the inevitable impact.

Then, two things happened. First, Berno swerved *sharp,* ripping off the road onto the shoulder, narrowly avoiding a collision with Marcus's bumper. At the same time, Berno slammed the brakes, his taillights glaring.

But Dakota had anticipated this. He heard a shout from the back seat, then the sudden roar of wind as she flung the back door open. She wasn't even buckled in, and Marcus's heart leapt in his throat at the sudden, reckless motion. Dakota was half-dangling out of the vehicle, given the exertion it had taken to shove the door. She hung over the asphalt, even as Marcus applied the brakes, the tires screeching.

Then, the door collided with Berno's bike where he'd been trying to slip past them on the shoulder.

A loud *thump.* A shout. Then the motorbike hit the floor in a shower of sparks. Marcus brought their own vehicle spinning around, his stomach in his throat, his shoulders jammed against the backrest from the motion. As they screeched in a circle, spinning, the scent of burning rubber and a cloud of smoke met the sparks from the scraped metal.

Then, briefly, everything went still.

Marcus still gripped the steering wheel with taught knuckles, his eyes like a deer in headlights. "Holy cow," he whispered. "You were right. I should've slowed." He blinked into the mirror where Dakota was still half-dangling out of the car, one hand braced against the handle where she'd forcefully flung it open. The window on the door had smashed from the impact with the bike. A large dent was visible in the silver metal, in the side mirror.

Dakota breathed heavily, her fingers shaking against the handle, her eyes staring towards the still road beneath her. If she'd fallen... If she'd slipped...

Agent Clement wet his dry lips, his nerves twisting in his stomach at the horrible possibilities cycling through his mind. “Drat,” he muttered beneath his breath. Was Dakota trying to get herself killed?

A moment later, though, he was distracted by the sudden sound of moaning coming from the side of the road. Berno's crumpled form twitched, then began to move. The man in the visored helmet tried to extricate himself from his toppled motorbike. His gloved hand twitched and his muscles displayed by the sleeveless shirt rippled as he moved for his gun once more.

“Stop!” Marcus shouted suddenly, shoving open his door and stumbling onto the roadside. “Hands in the air! Up! Up!”

Berno let out a series of expletives that caused Marcus to wince. But the biker let out a final, shuddering gasp and then raised one hand. “Can't move the other,” he moaned. “Don't shoot. Don't...”

“Stay right where you are!” Marcus shouted.

In the distance, he thought he vaguely heard the sound of wailing sirens.

“Berno, you're under arrest for the murder of Michayla Shirer!” Agent Clement said.

The man beneath his motorbike groaned again, his visored head tapping against the asphalt. “Shit,” he muttered, his voice muffled by the helm. His one good hand remained jutting in the air as Dakota moved from the back seat and Marcus approached, reaching for his handcuffs.

CHAPTER EIGHT

Dakota couldn't be sure why Marcus kept shooting her suspicious looks over the hospital bed, but she refused to give him the satisfaction of a reaction. Granted, the move with the door had been *somewhat* reckless, but he hadn't slowed the car when she'd said to. She'd known Berno was going to drop his speed. What else was she supposed to do? Just sit by and watch while a potential serial killer made good his getaway?

She wouldn't apologize. She refused. Marcus had been the one who'd *asked* for her help. This was it. She was helping.

And now, the two of them flanked the hospital bed. A nurse watched them disapprovingly from the door, having lodged far more than one complaint over the last few hours when they'd insisted that they be allowed to question the suspect.

He wasn't so injured he couldn't speak. So now, with two cops standing sentry outside the hospital room, and the two FBI agents crowding closer to the man on the bed, Bernardo Escoval didn't strike a particularly intimidating figure. In part, this was due to the cast over his left arm and the bandages along the side of his face. Plus, he was handcuffed to the bed.

"Mr. Escoval," Marcus said, finally redirecting his glare towards their suspect. "We ran your ID. You have an arrest record as long as my leg."

The man on the bed grunted, closing his eyes briefly. He had dark short-cut hair. A sharp nose and a masculine jawline. He was quite handsome, in Dakota's estimation. She could see why a girl like Michayla might fall for the act.

But now, having shot at two feds, lying in a hospital bed, the man's charms were somewhat lost on Dakota.

"Gun misfired," Berno said, his eyes still closed. "Was an accident. Didn't see you."

"That's your line, is it?" Marcus said with a snort. "A misfire?"

"That's what happened," Berno insisted.

Dakota crossed her arms, preferring to allow Clement to take the lead as he often did when it came to jawing. She preferred watching the suspects. Now, Escoval's jaw was tensed, his eyelids fluttering even when he kept them closed as if he were too discombobulated to be interviewed. She could see him thinking, though, far more alert than he wanted to let on. She glanced towards the morphine drip attached by IV to his left arm.

"And why did your gun misfire?" Clement pressed, his voice firm. "Was it because you were worried that we'd find these?" Dakota watched as her partner lifted the bag of white crystals, wiggling it in front of closed eyes. "You don't have to look," Marcus said. "But that's not going to change the facts."

Reluctantly, Berno's eyes half opened, remaining mostly hooded. He stared at the bag of crystal, then groaned, "Ain't mine. That's a plant."

Marcus snorted. "That's your tactic? The meth is a plant. Your gun misfired? You think a jury of your peers is going to believe you?"

Berno snorted, glancing off now towards the nurse as if looking for some backup. The woman in the door, though, was frowning towards the bag in Marcus's hand. "Excuse me," she protested. "What is *that*?"

Agent Clement sniffed, turning, and nodding politely. "Methamphetamine," he said simply. "More than a kilo. Enough to send Berno here away for a very, very long-time. That was *before* he tried to murder two FBI agents."

"You shouldn't have that in here," the nurse protested.

Marcus, gallant as ever, gave a quick nod and a smile. "We'll be out of your hair soon enough." He turned back towards their suspect. "It isn't looking good for you, Berno. If you cooperate now, it could go a long way in helping your sentence. I don't remember, Agent Steele, does Nevada have the death penalty?"

Berno winced at this, clicking his tongue and rapidly protesting. "Hang on—what? Shit—a little bit of crystal? What?"

"And shooting at cops," Marcus reminded, grim-faced.

"I missed! It was a misfire!"

"And murdering two young women, including your girlfriend, Michayla Shirer."

Berno suddenly tensed, staring. He swallowed, his tongue wetting his lips. His expression morphed now, his features shifting from scared to angry. "What the hell are you talking about? Mick? I—I thought I imagined you saying that. Shit. That was real? What happened to her?"

Dakota watched him like a hawk, studying his expression. The rigidity in his jawline had softened. His hand jutting from the cast had tensed. He winced in pain, though didn't seem to realize the clenching of his fist was causing this.

The signs of guilt? Confronted by his own evil?

The first two accusations he'd brushed off. The gunshots—a misfire. The drugs? A plant.

The murder, though? Anger. A question.

She just watched, tensed, waiting.

"Hey," Berno repeated, louder, "What the fuck happened to Mick!" His voice was rising now, his eyes bulging. Veins stood out on his neck above his sleeveless shirt collar as he began to hyperventilate. "You saying someone killed Mick? Are you saying someone killed her? What the hell! Hey! Hey what are you talking about?"

Marcus shot a quick look towards Dakota. This time a quizzical expression. She gave a faint, single-shoulder shrug, still watching. It was a very elaborate act. Dakota didn't enjoy beating around the bush. So instead, she took a more direct approach.

"Mr. and Mrs. Shirer seem to think you were involved in their daughter's death," Dakota said simply. "She was dragged to death behind a motorcycle. You ride a motorcycle. You were dating her. You also have an arrest record."

"For dealing! Are you batty!" His face was red now. His hand still tensed. "She's dead?" he said, his voice like a mewl. "Holy hell... how? When? Dragged? What do you mean dragged?"

The nurse in the door was now clicking her tongue disapprovingly. She cleared her throat, stepping into the room. "Please, agents, that's quite enough. You can see he's not able to—"

"Pardon, but one moment," Marcus interrupted, swiveling to face Berno once more. "When was the last time you saw Ms. Shirer?"

"I—she's dead?" his lip jutted petulantly now, like a child who's had a toy taken away. He shook his head, the bristles scraping against his cheap hospital pillow. "I—I didn't know nothing about that! I swear!"

"Yes. You've been very forthright with us."

"Forth what?"

"Means honest."

"Oh... oh—gun misfired."

"Exactly my point."

Berno was panicking now, sweat beading on his upper lip. "Shit—whatever else I might've done, I did *not* murder Mick. I liked Mick. She was a fun time man!"

"What a romantic. When was the last time you saw her?"

He huffed, shaking his head hurriedly. "I don't know. A few days? Five? Man she was talking all this stuff about getting back to her parents. Going back to school or some shit. I took a bit of a break. That was it. She woulda come back around. She always did."

"Some of that animal magnetism you possess, I imagine," Marcus said primly. Dakota hid a snort.

Berno didn't seem to realize he was being mocked. "That's what we are, ain't it? Animals? Naked apes. Well, I have urges, needs. Mick wasn't around so I shacked up with Cindy."

Marcus frowned now, pulling his small notebook from his pocket. "Hang on, Cindy? Who is that?"

"My new squeeze man. Hooker trolls *Nowhere.* Heard of it?"

"Yes, the biker bar."

"Right, well, Cindy was a good time. We been shacked up two days playing with each other and shooting...," he swallowed, quickly course correcting, "the breeze."

"Right—not shooting anything else. Certainly not into your veins?"

"Whadaya want from me, man. I didn't kill no one. Definitely not Mick. We was gonna have a threesome an' everything. Cindy was down for it. Why would I ruin that?"

His hand had uncurled now, and pale fingers rested against his chest, bent from the cast.

"This Cindy—can she vouch for you?" Marcus insisted.

"Man, course she can. Don't need her to, though. We was at that motel. Hour from here, by the way. Stuck there two days. Room 511. Call management, they'll tell you."

Marcus sighed. "What hotel?"

"Motel man. Not hotel. Do I look like Midas?"

"You know *Midas* but not forthright?"

"Man, I can read dude."

Marcus grimaced. "What was the name of the motel?"

"Hallows Inn," he retorted.

"Room number?" Marcus said innocently. But Dakota spotted the trap.

"Just told ya, dude. 511. Was there for two days."

No hesitation. He knew the room number he'd already given. Because he was telling the truth? Or because he'd rehearsed the lie?

Dakota felt a sudden jolt of unease in her stomach. She knew people, or at least tried to... This man seemed certain.

Out of the blue, she suddenly said, "Did you know Amber Reid, also?" She stared, watching his reaction.

But the man just wrinkled his nose. "Who?"

No sign of familiarity. Acting? Or maybe he really didn't know the first victim's name.

Marcus was watching her again, gauging her reaction. She passed a hand over her eyes, trying to think straight. She wanted nothing more than to find a liquor store and drink herself into a stupor. But it was too early—everything was still closed.

She felt her hands trembling and hid the effect by pressing them against her thighs. She didn't want to weigh-in. What if she was wrong? What if he really was the killer and she was being taken in by a clever act?

On the other hand...

She shivered. If she failed this one, like the last, another killer was going to get away. He abducted first, then killed. Just like the Motorcycle Murderer. If they didn't locate the real bastard, then another woman would inevitably die.

She shivered, rubbing her arms.

The *real* killer.

So that's what she thought. This wasn't it. They'd have to call the motel, have to follow the lead, but she was convinced. The alibi would check out. It wasn't Berno. He wasn't their man. He seemed genuinely shocked, disappointed, in a way a narcissist might be, at the news of Michayla's death.

He hadn't killed her. For all his flaws, he wasn't the serial killer.

She gave Marcus another look, and then a brief, grim jolting shake of her head. Agent Clement winced but didn't look surprised. He'd likely reached the same conclusion. Now, though, he was pulling his phone from his pocket.

"What was that motel's name again?" he said.

"I told you!" Berno shouted. "You wrote it down, man. What is this?"

"I'm going to call them, Berno. I'm going to track down Cindy. If any of them suggest you're lying, you won't just be looking at fifteen or so years for the drugs and the gunfire. You'll spend the rest of your life behind bars. Got me?"

"I didn't kill no one, man. And it was a misfire!"

"Just tell me the name of the motel. One more time."

As Berno continued to mutter protests, and the nurse in the door looked disapprovingly on, Dakota turned, shouldering past the nurse and moving towards the exit. She didn't want to just stand around any longer. She was sick of this.

Liquor stores wouldn't be open. But hotel mini-fridges—they might have what she needed. Besides, while Marcus was making some calls, she needed some sleep. A few more hours of rest. She had barely gotten any shut-eye over the stake-out. Just a quick few hours. They needed to find a hotel anyway, didn't they?

She pushed her trembling hand into her pocket, reaching for her own phone.

CHAPTER NINE

Before the lambs bleated, they often moved in silence. This was the rhythm of night. Again, his wheels rolled beneath him, a steady drone of rubber against road. He peered from beneath his visored helmet at the figure strolling the shoulder.

He watched the way her hips swayed, her legs stretched. Watched the way she moved. Even from behind, rolling slowly, he knew she was young. Twenties? Most likely. Dark hair. Didn't matter. The hair wasn't the important part.

No—he had more particular tastes. He'd already breezed past another woman, a few hours ago. She hadn't fit his type. And he did have a type. Not one he'd chosen, but one that had chosen him.

His eyes remained hooded behind his helmet, his face itching as it always did along the side of his cheek, down towards his chin. The scar-tissue always felt as if it were on fire. Pain did interesting things to a soul. Pain over the course of decades slowly chipped away at a man's sanity, like ocean waves against granite.

Even the strongest minds crumbled to pain.

For him it had taken two decades. For them, usually only two days. *Please kill me...*

He shivered at the words... the words he required them to speak. The only way out he offered. They usually came so full of bluster and brash and bravery. They felt they wouldn't break. But then he'd start. He'd play his games. Lonely, with him, no one else to hear the screams or intervene, they always sang a different tune.

Please kill me.

That was their safe word. That was his offer.

Once they said it, he was done. He stopped playing. He gave them their wish.

Now, as he rolled behind the strolling woman, admiring her figure, he wondered how long it might take for her to crack. *Please kill me.*

"As you wish," he whispered to himself, the sound of his hoarse voice lost in the growl of the engine.

He pulled ahead of the woman, a few paces away, giving her some space. He didn't want to scare her. That part came later. The fun was the reveal. No—fear could wait.

Now, he just needed a volunteer.

He came to a halt, twisting on his motorbike, his legs clasped against the vibrating seat and metal. His hands gripping the rubber guards. He allowed the bike to slow then lean, catching its weight on one foot after a couple of skipping steps. Once settled, he went completely still. Motionless. No gestures, no waving. It would be up to her now.

This was the test. The type. Some women were smart. Some of them made good choices. A ride from a stranger at night? Foolish. Everyone knew it... Except everyone didn't.

She hadn't. His own mother had been a stupid whore. A bitch with suds for brains.

Stupidity had to be punished. His mother had chosen a biker, too. About the same age as these idiots.

And so he waited—didn't say a word. Didn't want to spook nor entice. He wasn't here to make a sale's pitch. He was here to give an option. Part of him *hoped* she'd refuse. Hoped this little slut cat-walking on the shoulder of his highway was smart enough not to make an idiotic choice.

Sometimes they made good decisions.

But pitiably, more often than not, their estrogen-fueled idiocy came to light. Weaker sex indeed. Weak and stupid.

No words still. Just the rumble of the engine, the lonely, nighttime road. He kept his helmet in place. Partly because he didn't need to be identified, but also...

He gritted his teeth behind his visor, remembering the way women so often looked at him. Whispered. Pointed when they didn't think he was looking. Stupid bitches. Their fault he was disfigured in the first place! Their damn fault. He hadn't made the choice. His mother had. And so he now had half a face. A messed-up, scarred, monstrosity of a visage.

He gritted his teeth in frustration, feeling his rage mounting.

The woman had hesitated as he'd slowed, but now she was glancing towards the bike and then at the miles of empty highway ahead of her.

"Did you see my car back there?" she said, calling out, her voice nearly lost in the engine's growl.

He didn't move. He'd spotted her stupid little Prius. A west coast car if ever there was one. And now she was intimidated by the walk. Lazy *and* stupid. He could feel it in his bones. This whore would volunteer.

Pity, too. A new whore meant the old one had to go. *Please kill me.* His last captive would eventually utter those words. He'd just have to increase the pressure given this new volunteer.

And he was right. He could always spot the type.

The bitch hesitated a moment, glanced at his silent silhouette. It was still dark, thanks to the mountains, as the sun slowly climbed. Barely morning.

He just waited, patient, quiet. He had all the time in the world. Little did she know, her own fate was in her hands. He never forced them to choose the bike. Never forced them to join him. Only once they chose—then their fate was sealed.

"Alright," the woman said finally with a smile and a flounce. "Thanks mister. I appreciate it."

She approached. It took her a couple of tries to even straddle the bike. Clumsy and ditzy and stupid and a whore and—JUST GET ON THE DAMN BIKE!

His simmering rage boiled over briefly, and he gave her a faint tug, pulling her on the vehicle behind him. As his gloved hand touched her exposed arm, she flinched. But only for a second. Once she sat steady, tentatively, her arms reached out, pressing on his shoulders. Not so tight. That would come later. Once he picked up speed. They always tightened their grip.

They didn't have a choice.

Even now, the choice had vanished. She didn't know it yet, but as he began to pick up speed, he allowed himself a faint chuckling laugh. Even this was disguised by the growling engine and the vibrating motorbike. Her hands gripped tighter on his shoulders.

Thank you, mister.

Three words. Such ignorant words. Soon, she'd be uttering three others.

But first, his most recent capture would speak first. He'd dispose of the old and bring in the new. Her frail little hands gripped his shoulders tighter as they continued to pick up speed. Faster, faster. She was trying to say something now, tensed. But he never listened to them.

What could a woman say that was worth listening to anyway?

He'd deal with his last capture, dump her somewhere nearby and then start on this new little idiot.

Around and around the cycle went, just like the wheels on his bike.

CHAPTER TEN

It hadn't been difficult to find a hotel. She'd received a couple of strange glances from the desk clerk while checking in so early in the morning and requesting no room service. Now, though, laying on the queen-sized bed, her eyes closed, Dakota felt her thoughts drifting. A couple of the small bottles clinked together where they rolled at the foot of her bed.

The mini-fridge was already half empty.

At least she didn't have to share a room next to Marcus. He was shacked up on the floor above hers. A mercy. She didn't need to worry about him listening in on her own business. Besides, a few drinks here and there only helped things. It wasn't like she was hurting anyone.

She shifted again, holding back a burp that would taste of bourbon and nothing else. The bottles on her nightstand were stacked like sentries. The two she hadn't managed to find still clinked somewhere in the vicinity of her feet.

She pulled the blanket tight, wincing against the sunlight drifting through the blinds over the bed. She'd asked for a room facing the alley, but they'd only had this one. Staring straight at the rising sun. Early morning or not, she always found it difficult to sleep without darkness.

She'd only be able to get a few hours before having to rise and face the rest of the day—hopefully, a few hours of shut-eye in the morning wouldn't completely throw off her sleep schedule.

Then again... who was she kidding.

She hadn't had anything like a schedule for the last three months.

And as her mind went hazy, as the fog descended, she was reminded exactly why.

The nightmare started as faint, trailing thoughts leaving behind tethers of consciousness. Carol, sea-gray eyes, dimpled cheeks, the echoing little giggle.

She could just about see her sister in the dark space behind her eyelids. She wanted to reach out. She murmured, shifting—no longer hearing the clink of glass. No longer feeling the bed or the faint warmth of sunlight creeping through the blinds.

All she felt was cold.

And terror.

Prickles pattered up her spine with zeal. Her mind tried to flee, vying to retreat. But too late... Another faint giggle—a flash of gray eyes.

She stumbled on something.

Dakota cursed, reeling back in this place between sleep and horror. A body on the ground. A small, crumpled form like a wilted flower, discarded so easily. The little pink stencils of roses on the backpack straps stood out against the bleak floor.

The blood stained the pink flowers. Stained the ground. Those sea gray eyes weren't smiling anymore but stared up like glass. The smile was gone.

Horror welled in Dakota's chest as she stared at Carol's lifeless form. She ripped her gaze away, hyperventilating—or not breathing at all. She couldn't be sure.

You'll never find me... A voice whispered in her mind.

The voice sounded how the prickles on her back felt. A strange comparison but the two sensations originated from the same depraved hellhole. *I'm gone... gone... the wind took me. The dust is all that's left...*

"SHUT UP!" she screamed, no attempts at disguising her emotions now. No ability to. "Shut up!" she repeated, clenching her hands at her side. But her fingers felt so weak, her mind so fuzzy.

She could still feel her little sister lying on the ground. Could see the blood speckling the backpack's straps. Could feel those accusing, lifeless eyes staring up at her. Why hadn't Dakota walked her home? Why hadn't she been there?

Almost twenty-five years now she'd tried to outrun the horrible events of that night. She remembered being sent to detention for getting into a fight. Her sister had walked home alone.

The monster had taken her from just down the street.

You'll never find me.... The voice whispered. *I'm the wind.*

She tried to scream again, but her tongue stuck to the roof of her mouth. She spun around, but everything was gray. Was dark. Mist swelled in, rolling like a wave to the shore. Dead. Dead. Vanished. Like the wind.

The taunting voice faded. The images faded. And now all she experienced was darkness. She was alone. Isolated in a room of mist and murk. No one to hear her cry or scream. No one to care if she did neither. She was alone.

Always had been. She'd failed her sister. Failed Carol the same way she'd failed the case from three months ago. Two souls she could've saved. Should have. But her own stupid ego had cost it all.

She shivered now, crumpling in on herself in the dark dream. Her arms clasped over her trembling knees, and she let out a shaking sob. A tear traced inside her cheek, and her body ached for something—anything to numb it all.

And then a shrill beep suddenly woke her.

Dakota blinked, head tensing against the hotel room pillow. Her foot hit something glassy and cold. Another noise—a ring, not a beep. Her phone from the nightstand.

Dakota let out a faint warbling groan but reached out, trying to drag at the phone with trembling fingers. She could still feel the tears in her eyes. Angrily she wiped them with the blanket before answering the phone in a shaky voice, hiding her irritation so quickly that no signs were left of her terror, her sleeplessness, her grief.

"Hello," she said in a polite but casual tone. The horrible thoughts, the feelings faded as she said it, disappearing as quickly as they'd come.

"Agent Steele?" the voice on the line said.

"Acting agent," she corrected. She lowered the phone to give herself a chance to let out a shaking breath. But steadying, she lifted it in time to hear.

"This is Deputy Watkins. Sheriff said I should call. We found another body. How soon can you be here?"

Dakota frowned, staring across her dark room. She hesitated for a moment, wondering if she ought to just get back on a plane and return to Rapid City.

"Hello? Agent Steele?"

She closed her eyes, biting back the response she wanted to give. An apology followed by a quick exit. But then, she growled and said, biting the words, "Text me an address. We'll be there right away."

Sleep would have to wait.

It was happening again.

Another body.

Another woman dead.

It was all happening again.

***

Noon only barely arrived as Dakota slipped out of the back seat, not even glancing towards Agent Clement as her feet seemed to roll across the dusty ground of their own accord. Her eyes fixated on the young woman who appeared to be resting against the metal post. Her legs splayed in the grass, her feet bare and pointing towards the desert skies. The brown, scruffy layer of prickling grass was interspersed by thorns and bitter weeds with prickles. And yet the woman sat, her back to the metal traffic barrier, her eyes open, staring off.

It almost looked as if she'd just stopped after a long journey, taking a brief respite.

But the illusion of life was ruined the closer Dakota neared. The woman's face was a mess. Scrape marks and deep gouges, from where she'd been dragged across the road, embedded in her features. Blood, dry now, caked her face, her sweater, her arms. Her sweater was ripped, same as her pants. The sweater, though, judging by the tag which Dakota noticed instantly, was on backwards. As if it had been removed then replaced haphazardly.

The young woman's head was tilted on her neck, almost quizzically. More likely, this was due to a broken spine.

A couple of forensic units were scurrying about the scene, gloves on, cameras in hand, evidence bags being labeled and stowed for further examination.

"Alison Beswick," called a voice from behind her. "Twenty-one years old. Her boyfriend was the last one to see her."

Dakota listened vaguely and gave brief nod. "When did she go missing?" she asked, her voice shaky. Her thumbs were tucked in her pockets again, her fingers drumming rhythmically against her thigh.

The deputy who'd driven them cleared his throat, asphalt crunching as he drew alongside her. "A day ago," he murmured. "According to her boyfriend, who we're interviewing now, they had an argument and she stalked off. He says she probably tried to hitch a ride."

Dakota nodded faintly. This fit with their assessment of the previous victim also.

She stared down at the corpse of Ms. Beswick, studying the way the body had been placed, posed even. Such a lackadaisical, carefree posture. What did it mean? Why did he take them—then drag these women to their deaths behind his motorbike? Judging by the dust, the bits of gravel, the horrible wounds, he didn't just drag them on highways or roads, but off-terrain too. Perhaps even the desert.

She heard Marcus clear his throat behind her. He hadn't drawn in line with her yet, preferring to survey the scene at a distance. His tone was grim—gone was his usually cheerful entreaties. Gone was his ever-professional demeanor. Now, he just sounded angry. "She went missing a day ago and we find her now. Seems reasonable to assume he's holding them. Like we predicted."

Dakota nodded once. She waved towards the sweater. "Her clothing is backwards."

She didn't connect the dots. Agent Clement could do it himself. The two of them drifted off into grim silence. Dakota studied the corpse, refusing to look away, her eye on the details, the posture, anything that might hint at the man who'd done this.

Agent Clement, though she wasn't watching at him, was likely studying the terrain, or the ground, preferring to look in any direction but the corpse itself. He was too kind, too empathetic to properly focus on the victim. It hurt him to study the dead. It angered him.

This was one of the reasons they'd both taken it so personally three months ago. She wondered if Clement blamed her still... She could still remember him shouting... *I told you!*

She let out a shivering sigh. She dropped to her haunches, the faint odor of fetid meat decaying beneath the sun now stinging her nostrils. "Do we have any other missing persons reports in the last couple of days?" she asked faintly.

The deputy behind her cleared his throat. "Ah—one moment."

She heard him shift as if turning away, followed by the static sound of a radio. Briefly, the sound of murmuring from forensics, the muted sound of footsteps or crumpling bags or heavy breathing hung over the roadside. After a few muttered comments from the deputy and an answering voice over the radio, Dakota felt the man step nearer to her, drawing her attention.

She glanced up at the officer.

"A couple, but only one young woman."

"When?"

"Early this morning, or late last night," he said. "However you think about it. Highway patrol found her car abandoned. Didn't find her though."

Dakota frowned. "Name?"

"Miranda Lopez. Twenty-six. She was driving an Eclipse. Engine trouble. No sign of her."

"And this was last night?"

"Not more than eight hours ago. They spoke to Mrs. Lopez's husband. He said she was driving home late from a conference."

Dakota pushed shakily back to her feet, her legs tight as she moved.

"Makes sense... Interesting..."

Marcus leaned in next to her, his shadow cast over her by the sun. "What are you thinking?"

"I'm thinking... our killer took a new victim. And he disposed of his last one."

"What does that mean?"

She turned to face the gentle giant, removing her frown and keeping her emotions in check as ever. She touched briefly at her turtleneck, making sure the tattoos beneath were still hidden. She cleared her throat. Then, as dispassionately as possible, she rattled off, "He's taking them one at a time it seems. If he gets a new one, he kills the old one. He's probably raping them. Maybe torture. He drags them to their death to disguise and obscure physical evidence, but also more than that—he likes humiliating them. Likes hurting them."

She glanced back at the body, wincing. "Chances are he starts slow. I doubt the process is quick."

"You think he kills his victims if he catches a new one?" Marcus said, frowning. "Essentially replacing them? Why?"

"Why one at a time? I don't know. Maybe so he can direct his full attention...," she trailed off, then corrected herself, "His full *rage* towards a single individual." She glanced towards the corpse, a lance of sadness jolting through her. "So much rage," she murmured.

"That means...," Marcus said, "We have to find him before he finds another captive. Otherwise, Ms. Lopez is as good as dead too."

The deputy interjected now, speaking quickly in a burst of words as if he'd been waiting for the right moment.

"We have the boyfriend's address. The sheriff spoke to him earlier. There's evidence from the neighbors the relationship could get violent."

Dakota quirked an eyebrow. "He doesn't happen to drive a motorcycle, does he?"

"Umm, no. Looks like he drives a truck."

"Well—a violent boyfriend of Ms. Beswick is as good a place as any to start, I suppose," Dakota said, nodding. Inwardly, she could feel the darkness pressing in. The nightmare still haunted the inside of her eyelids, insisting itself in her brain.

She gritted her teeth in frustration but pushed past the horror. "We need to borrow the car," she said towards the deputy. "Also, we need the boyfriend's address."

"Yeah... that's the thing," the deputy said. "He's not actually local. Doesn't really have an address. He's staying at a motel, though. That's where we spoke to him."

"An itinerant boyfriend who is violent?"

"Yeah. Other guests at the motel, the neighbors above and to the left both heard shouts and the sound of blows. I can send you the full report if you like."

"Great. Send it. And make sure they keep him at the motel until we get there. Don't want him bolting without a babysitter."

She turned her back to the corpse, only then feeling the icy knot in her stomach as, stiff-legged, she marched away, back in the direction of the squad car.

CHAPTER ELEVEN

Line Six Inn found itself smack dab between a truck stop and a chain fast food restaurant. Grease, cheap beef, and diesel fuel wafted on the air over the small, single-story structure—the large wooden sign boasting fading white letters above reception.

Gray doors settled the dusty, white walls. And Dakota spotted where two cops were lounging by room 132 as Marcus pulled into a parking spot.

Dakota examined the dusty, gray doors of the motel, her eyes skipping. What she had taken for a single-story structure, proved to be more than met the eye. Sections of the motel had railings which led up to a second level. The different, protruding second story gave the roadside motel a look like castle battlements.

As Marcus pulled their borrowed vehicle to a stop, put it in park and threw open the door, the two police officers stationed outside their suspect's room glanced over curiously.

Dakota allowed Marcus to take the lead this time, walking stiff-legged across the asphalt towards the babysitters.

"Agent Clement," Marcus said, flashing his ID. "Our suspect still inside?"

The two cops bobbed their heads. One of them, a blonde-haired young man with a scraggly goatee muttered, "Not sure how coherent he's going to be."

Marcus frowned. "What does that mean?"

"Nothing. Just, he's been drinking."

Dakota stiffened at this. Her stomach twisted. Perhaps she was reading too much into it, but the deputy seemed to have a note of contempt in his voice.

"Would still like to chat," Agent Clement said.

The blonde cop shrugged, stepped towards the door, knocked a couple of times, then tried the handle.

It opened. The cop pulled it wider and gestured towards the agents.

The stench of body odor and sweat erupted from inside the motel. Dakota waved a hand in front of her face. She glanced inside the motel room and spotted discarded pizza boxes and bottles across the ground.

Piles of clothes in one corner. A bed with the mattress on the floor. Everything was a mess. Inwardly, she screamed for orderliness. Her normal compulsive tendencies when it came to hygiene and tidiness rebelled. The pathetic figure of the late victim's boyfriend was draped over the mattress on the ground. He held a bottle in one hand, pointed towards his eye as if he was trying to examine the insides. Most likely investigating where all the alcohol had vanished to.

Dakota felt the cops shift behind her. Marcus cleared his throat, shot her a quick look of concern, but then hid it as a cough.

She knew he was just concerned for her. But that look alone caused her cheeks to redden. The pathetic figure inside the dark, stinky, trashed motel room caused her face to warm further. Was this how others saw her?

The pity, the repulsion, the disgust... And even now, as shame coursed down her spine, all she could really think about was the opportunity to get another drink of her own. How pathetic was that?

She jammed her thumbs inside her pockets, her right-hand clenching into a fist. But there was nothing to fight except herself. And in that case no amount of training seemed to help.

"You good?" Marcus murmured at her side.

In answer, she stepped through the motel room door, marching towards the prone figure.

"Mr. Maguire," she called out, breathing determinedly through her mouth to avoid inhaling the horrific stench.

The man on the mattress waved his bottle above his head. A couple of droplets splattered his chin. Not the only liquid that had drenched his form.

"Get out," he yelled. "I'm grieving."

The man on the ground wore boxers and not much else. He had a bit of a beer belly, and pepperoni sized nipples also sloshed with beer. His face was ruddy and red. Sweat droplets speckled his brow. He was groaning as he tried to sit up. Once, twice, he threw his hips to rise, but his muscles weren't strong enough. So in the end, he let out a long groan as he shoved off his side, shimmying up the wall with his back, and now sitting on the mattress and facing them with a glare. The way he reclined against the wall, his legs splayed beneath him, reminded Dakota of how they had found the victim posed back on the side of the road. Again, her shame faded to be replaced by a more sober-minded analytical approach. This was a man who'd been seen with the most recent victim. A violent man according to witnesses. Could he be their suspect? Or was he just a witness?

"Mr. Maguire, we're with the FBI," Dakota said, grimacing at how easily the words spilled from her tongue. "We need to speak with you about your girlfriend."

"She's been taken," he said, then burped. "By that guy on the news—the dirt bike strangler, or whatever. Let me grieve."

Dakota crossed her arms. "I have a few questions that might help us find who did this."

"I've already answered questions."

Dakota shot a look back towards the open doorway where the cops were leaning in and watching. Agent Clement stood just behind her, allowing her to take charge. She returned her attention towards their witness. "We heard from some of the neighbors that you had a habit of getting violent with Ms. Beswick. Is that true?"

To her surprise, he didn't deny it. He just nodded, glumly. He waved to the bottle in his hand like a scepter. "It's this damn stuff," he said. "Best of friends. Worst of enemies." He nodded as if he had just said the most sage thing ever recorded. He gave an imperious little tilt of his head, but the effect was somewhat ruined by the subsequent burp.

"You also mentioned in your previous questioning that you'd gotten into a fight with Alison before she disappeared."

"An argument. She broke up with me."

"Why did she break up with you?"

He stared at her, glanced at the palm of his hand, and his cheeks suddenly reddened. "What are you saying?" He slurred. The round-faced Maguire suddenly crossed his arms, tucking his legs under him. He looked small and cold all of a sudden.

Dakota pressed, "I'm just asking questions. Did you know Amber Reid?"

“Who?”

“How about Michayla Shirer?”

“Nah, man. Don't know her.”

“Are you sure? You don't recognize her?” Dakota flashed a driver's license photo of the second victim on her phone. The man just stared at it, his eyes glazed. He burped, then turned away with a groan.

"I miss her already,” he moaned. “I missed her the moment she left. I should've treated her better," he said, with a small sad shake. He took another sip from his already empty bottle. When he realized it was dry, in order to save pride, if such a thing were possible, he pretended to swallow as if there had been alcohol in it all along.

"Can you tell us anything else about Alison? When she went missing, what happened after?"

"I got pissed, drove back here. Got a drink. I don't know what happened to her. Now I wish I'd gone looking." He sniffed, shaking his head.

"So when she broke up with you, where was that?"

"Gas station. A desert road. I don't know."

Dakota sighed. "And you didn't see her after?"

"Not a bit. I came right back here. You mentioned those nosy neighbors. Well, that big fat lady upstairs saw me. Ask her."

Dakota made a mental note to check his story. But as she looked at the man, it didn't really make sense. He didn't seem to own a motorcycle, for one. She'd seen pictures of the truck registered to him. There was no bike attached to his license. Secondly, he was in such a state, there was no way he could've even driven in a straight line. And finally, the motel was small, cramped, with nosy neighbors. If the killer really was capturing women and torturing them before killing them, he would need somewhere more private, away from the scrutiny of other motel dwellers. This was just a sad, miserable man. Not their killer. But also, very little help.

"Does Alison have family in the area?"

"Family? Hell no. She was alone, like me. That's what hit us off."

"Where is her family?"

"Doesn't have any. Not anymore. She grew up kind of normal, both her parents died a couple of years ago. Car crash. We met at the funeral."

"I'm very sorry to hear that."

"Whatever, lady. Alison was an angel." His eyes suddenly burned with tears, and his shoulders began to shake. Dakota looked away. Marcus watched the man, a faint look of compassion on his face. A strange contrast. Back at the crime scene, she'd stared at the corpse, but Marcus had looked away. Now here in the motel room, it was the reverse.

She didn't have anything else to add. The man wasn't in any state to go around killing people. He was just a drunk. A violent one.

Just a drunk. She shivered, turning on her heel and pushing back through the door. She could hear agent Clement murmuring something softly. "Is there anything I can get you, sir?"

But even this tone of mercy from her partner curdled Dakota's belly. Was that why he had invited her? Pity? She wasn't anything like that guy. Was she?

She crossed her arms tightly, hugging her sweater and shooting a long look towards the nearest cop.

"You guys looped into what's been going on?"

The sandy haired officer nodded. "We're keeping the radio open."

"What channel is the sheriff on?"

The cop hesitated, shared a look with his partner, but then pulled his own radio from his belt and handed it to her.

Dakota accepted it with a quick nod.

She clicked the radio, waited, then said, "This is acting Agent Steele. Come in."

A pause, then static. She waited, then tried again. She listened, and only then did she hear a vague voice. "Agent Steele?"

She pictured the older man with the military haircut. "Yes, sir," she said. “We're a no go on the dead woman's boyfriend. We were told you were tracking down the most recent victim's husband. Do we have information on Mr. Lopez yet?"

"Yes. Will send it over. He lives out of state, apparently.”

She frowned. “Wait, really? Why was his wife here?”

“You can ask him via video. Hang tight. And Agent Steele, don't use this line."

It clicked off. She shrugged sheepishly, handing the device back to the officer. Marcus stepped onto the porch behind them, shutting the door gently.

"We're going to need to check with the neighbors," Clement said, "to see when he was here."

The cops both nodded to show they heard. "It's not him," Dakota said stiffly. "He's useless.”

"I wouldn't say he's useless," Marcus said quickly. "He's hurting. I get it."

She shot him a look, eyes narrowed. Was he trying to proxy pity her? But Marcus was staring at the back of his hands, refusing to look her in the eye.

Proxy pity indeed.

She muttered, "Mrs. Lopez's husband might know something more useful. The sheriff's gonna send us his information."

"Right," Marcus said.

"Just one thing," Dakota replied, frowning, "the sheriff said he lives out of state. We're going to have to speak with him by video."

***

Dakota stared at the high-definition image on her partner's phone. The two of them were leaning towards the dash between them, over the gearshift, twin frowns creasing their brows as they peered down at the device. Marcus had to stoop a bit further, given his substantial height advantage.

The image stuttered briefly, but then resumed, crisp and clear, revealing a man in a suit, sitting dazed on a couch. A police officer stood off behind him, speaking in hushed tones on his own phone. The couch had tasseled arms and tasteful throw pillows. A small child, no older than two, wiggled on the couch, playing with one of the pillows and occasionally looking up towards the wide-eyed man.

Mr. Lopez looked shell-shocked, not that Dakota could blame him. He had salt-and-pepper hair, with olive skin and long eyelashes. He would have looked handsome if not for his disheveled appearance and his red-ringed eyes.

"Pardon?" he murmured into his phone, blinking. "What was the question?"

Dakota cleared her throat. "I asked how far from San Francisco you live."

"About an hour's drive," he murmured.

"And your wife—we were told she was in Nevada for a conference."

"Yes... yes for work. She coordinates restaurant franchises." He waved a hand but lowered it to catch the child who was now trying to crawl over the back of the couch. As his hand touched his son's leg, pulling him back to safety, Dakota glimpsed a surge of grief which the man swallowed. "I—I should've called sooner. When she didn't call to tuck Miggy in." He stroked his hand through his son's hair. The small boy nuzzled up under his father's arm, staring at the camera now as well, his large, brown eyes searching the object of his father's apparent interest. He stared off, his eyes carrying a distant quality. "She's traveled to Nevada before for work. I never thought...." he swallowed. "Never considered she might...." he let out a shaky sigh, then looked directly into the camera. "Do you know who did this? Where she is? They wouldn't tell me." He shot a vengeful look towards the cop on a call behind his couch. "Who took her?"

"We're working on it," Dakota interjected. "Your wife... was she disconnected from her family? Did she have a troubled past?"

“What? No—why would you think that?”

“Just trying to narrow parameters.”

“My wife loves her family. They live five minutes from us. She was valedictorian at her school. Graduated from UOD with distinctions. Please, can you at least tell me if she's...,” he swallowed and mouthed the word, *alive.*

The young boy on his lap was reaching up to pet at his father's chin, mercifully ignorant of the atmosphere in the room and over the call.

Dakota leaned back in the car seat, frowning as Marcus started working through a more conventional questionnaire, starting once more with the basics. But the woman's identity wasn't going to help. That much was clear. The killer had abducted a drifter, a hitchhiker. He'd gone after the marginalized—young women in their twenties without family connections.

But this time... Ms. Lopez's car had broken down on the side of the road.

A crime of opportunity. Nothing more.

The killer was hunting anyone he could find. His type was young women—that was it. Socio-economic status, family connections, vulnerability—it didn't matter in the way they'd first expected.

Dakota blinked, glancing back towards the screen in her partner's hand, watching the wide-eyed husband and his two-year-old son set against the couch. She wondered what the boy would think once he learned his mother was missing.

Dakota found her hand bunching in her lap. She couldn't let that happen. She had to find this monster before he killed Ms. Lopez. Right now, she was going through hell, but there was still a chance they could get her back before it was too late.

She muttered beneath her breath, “I'll be right back.”

Marcus protested, “Hang on—where are you going?”

“Just stretching my legs. I'll be back quick. It's fine.”

She didn't wait for a response. Instead, she pushed open the car door, stepping back out in front of the seedy motel they'd parked in front of. The two cops guarding the first-level room were leaning against the wall with hooded eyes. Dakota didn't look towards them, didn't look towards the motel room door.

She could feel Marcus watching her. Could feel the suspicion in his gaze. She hesitated, wondering if she ought to offer an excuse. But then she jammed her thumbs into her pocket, her hands pressed against her thighs, and, stiff-legged, she marched away from the parked car, along the street next to the motel. Ahead, she spotted a gas station.

She swallowed, her throat feeling dry all of a sudden, her head pounding. Darkness pressed around her, and her heart hammered as she picked up the pace, trying to distance herself from Marcus's watchful gaze and her own nagging conscience.

CHAPTER TWELVE

Dakota stood outside the gas station, under the noonday sunlight. She shifted uncomfortably, kicking a stray aluminum can skittering across the ground. She peered through the smudged, glass window at the white-bearded man behind the counter. He resembled an Indian Santa Claus with crinkled eyes and bushy, well-trimmed facial hair. Her eyes skipped to the selection of bottles behind the counter.

Whiskey was on the top shelf. Her poison of choice, though, was the straight tequila. The clear, blue bottles of the cheapest brand were in the middle of the display case.

Eyes hooded, she peered through the glass, staring at the siren's call of the motionless bottles. She deserved a bit of a break, didn't she? It had been a long day. Well... she glanced at the mid-day sun... at least a long *half* day.

It had been a while since she'd downed an entire bottle in one sitting... She could practically feel her brain firing at the thought of it, her body already growing excited at the prospect. What was the point of coming here, anyway? She knew what made her happy. The only thing that numbed it all, that helped her forget.

It came cheap in South Dakota, the same as Nevada. And in the former, alone in her apartment, there wasn't nearly so much guilt. She licked her lips, catching the motion in the middle and going still. She wondered how others might think of her if they could see inside her brain. She reached out towards the cold metal handle of the gas station door. Her fingers grazed the surface, and she was surprised to see her hand trembling. The Santa Claus attendant hadn't noticed her yet. He was busy helping an older woman check out with a bag of Sun Crisps.

Dakota didn't open the door at first. She simply stood there, hand extended, uncertain what to do. *How* to do it. It seemed like a crossroads. But not an unfamiliar branching path, rather an all-too familiar one. A million times she'd had the option to choose the other branching path, but no matter which road she set out on, she was given a million more chances to change her mind.

It was all so exhausting.

She just wanted to sleep... to forget. To never dream again.

She wanted to drift away. To lose herself.

She flinched, half opening the door. A warm breeze emanated from the heated building, carrying the scent of dust and burnt hot dogs. She held the door half ajar. Part of her was fighting the decision. The same part of her that always fought against overwhelming odds. The same part that had always kept her safe. Had protected her.

But she was just so damn tired of it all. Tired of remembering, tired of trying, tired of walking incessantly up a mountain with no peak.

She glanced again towards the second shelf with the cheap, blue bottles. She gritted her teeth, summoning courage and suddenly reached a decision, yanking the door open.

It didn't budge. It jerked a foot but then jarred to a halt.

She pulled again, more urgently. This time, the door slammed shut.

And then she saw the large hand above her head, holding the door shut. The fingers smudged the glass, and she traced the hand to a muscled arm. Her eyes trailed to meet the downturned face of Agent Marcus Clement.

She stared into his eyes for a moment. He stared back. Like that, his hand braced against the glass door, hers pressed loosely to the handle, they stood motionless, eye-to-eye. She swallowed and he exhaled.

At last, she found her nerve. “Let go, Marcus,” she said, her tone even.

“How's it going Steele,” he replied softly.

“Let go of the door, big guy.”

“I'd really rather not.”

“Marcus...,” she trailed off, allowing a bit of a growl into her tone.

“Recalcitrant,” he murmured. “Do you know what it means?”

“Marcus, I'm not in the mood for one of your word games. Get your hand off the damn door. Now!” Her temper suddenly surged, taking even herself off guard. She blinked and tried to bite back the vitriol. But Marcus didn't budge.

“And if I do, what will you do then? Tequila, right? That's your favorite.”

She blinked as if she'd been slapped. Something about the utterance of the word made her skin crawl. “I don't owe you an explanation,” she whispered, her voice faint. “Let go of the damn door.”

“I just want to know. Which bottle? I can get it for you, myself. How about that, hmm? I'll buy it. My treat. Vodka? Whiskey? Fireball? I hear that's like liquid candy.” He spoke conversationally, lackadaisical even, but his eyes held acid.

"I don't need your help, Clement. Get out of my way before...."

"Before what, hmm? Are you going to punch me? That'd be interesting, wouldn't it? Sheer size against decades of training. I'd pay to see that fight."

She breathed heavily, inhaling and exhaling so loudly she couldn't hear herself think. She wanted to turn and run and hide. She wanted to drive her fist into Marcus's stupid face. She wanted to snatch a couple of bottles and down them in a single go. She wanted to forget it all, to hide.

But there he was, standing over her like some guardian angel or perhaps just a leering gargoyle, watching her every move, like a spotlight. She couldn't hide. Couldn't pretend, couldn't flee.

She swallowed, her throat thick with emotion. She wanted to cry now. "I don't want to fight you," she murmured in a ghost of a whisper. "I don't..."

"I know," he whispered back. "Dakota, you don't need to be here. Alright? Not right now. Not today."

He lowered his hand slowly, his eyes misty, though he tried to hide it by looking away. "It's going to be okay," he murmured. "We can still help them. We can help *her.*"

"She's dead, Marcus," Dakota whispered. "She's dead."

"Miranda Lopez isn't," he retorted, his voice fierce. He reached down, wrapping an enormous arm around her small shoulders. Not a forceful motion. She tensed at first, but his hands were warm against her arm as he gently tried to nudge her away, guiding her from the door back in the direction of the parking lot.

She went rigid, and he didn't force her movement. At last, though, she let out a shuddering sigh and allowed him to guide her slowly away, leading her back down the street.

She wanted to look back. Wanted to peer through that gas station window once more. But she didn't want to fight Marcus. Besides, he was right.

It wasn't too late for Ms. Lopez.

Not yet.

She couldn't take another body on her conscience.

It would shatter her.

"We need another angle," she murmured faintly. "If we're going to help her, we have to think of something else. The victims aren't connected. They're opportunistic."

Marcus sighed. "I was thinking the same thing. See—that insight right there is why I brought you, Agent Steele. So if not a connection between the victims, then what?"

She paused briefly, let out another faint sigh then said, "The killer." She moved along the sidewalk with a slow rolling step, her mind still on fire, her thoughts still cloudy. "We have to find the killer."

"Yeah... and where should we start with that, Agent Steele?"

"Stop calling me that. Just... just stop it."

"No," Marcus said primly. "Just because you don't know who you are, doesn't mean I'm going to join your ignorance." He didn't say it to rebuke her but stated it matter-of-factly.

She sighed in resignation, but then said, "Killers and ex-cons operating in the same radius as our guy. Cross-reference with DMV records of motorcycle riders. Might get us a list to start with at least."

Marcus blinked, but then nodded. "Perfect. I'll call the office. We can set up a secure connection from a hotspot in the car."

"Right—tell them to hurry. This guy is escalating. We need to find him before he gets tired of Ms. Lopez. Before he...." She trailed off, her gaze haunted, staring into the distance. She moved like a woman in a dream, allowing Marcus to pick up the pace, guiding her hurriedly back towards their waiting vehicle. At the same time, Agent Clement pulled his phone from his pocket in order to call the BAU office for the required permissions and access to the necessary databases to catch their killer.

***

They were back in the car, and Dakota felt uncomfortable. She kept fidgeting, adjusting her position in the passenger seat, and occasionally glancing in Marcus's direction, trying to keep an eye on the large agent. His laptop screen was open, and now, as they'd connected to the BAU database, he was typing to narrow their search parameters.

"Fifty-mile radius sound good?" he muttered.

"Make it seventy-five," she returned, still not quite meeting his gaze. She looked up through the window, once again scanning the parking lot outside the motel.

Marcus was pretending like nothing had happened. Pretending like he hadn't just physically prevented Dakota from buying alcohol. Pretending like everything was back to normal. In the past, she'd battled her drinking and Marcus hadn't brought it up. In the past, it hadn't prevented her from doing her job. Now, she wondered if things were only escalating.

"All right," he said. "Seventy-five. Got it. What else?"

"The criminal record, tweak it for violence against women specifically. Assault alone will be too broad."

"Attempted murder?"

"Included. But don't limit to it."

Marcus flashed a thumbs up, but then returned to typing rapidly. He could type very fast. Partly because of his experience with computers, but also, she knew, because on the side, Marcus liked to write stories.

"Have anything?" she asked.

Marcus held a finger as the search bar swam. The two of them waited, both staring towards the circling icon in the middle of the screen.

The rising sun, directly above them now, heated the windows, and took the place of the chill wind from the night. The desert sands rapidly heated during the day, and then cooled when evening fell. Now, Dakota tugged at her turtleneck, wishing they had the air conditioning unit running.

But before she could lodge a complaint, she was distracted by the sudden appearance on her screen.

"A couple hundred names," Marcus reported. "All narrowed based on motorcycle owners. Hang tight. I'm using traffic infractions."

Dakota just waited, with bated breath.

Her partner hit enter. And then a new list appeared. Five names.

She felt her stomach lurch. "Not that one," she said quickly, tapping the screen.

Marcus leaned in, frowning, but then realized the issue—a 72-year-old man wasn't likely to drag young, athletic women to their deaths behind his bike. Wasn't likely to overpower anyone.

"Or that one," Dakota said.

"Why not?"

"Female. You didn't narrow by gender."

Marcus cursed and readjusted the settings.

Now, there were only two names remaining.

"This one is still in prison," Marcus said, tapping a finger beneath a highlighted name.

“So that leaves us with... Demar Ramsey,” Dakota murmured, peering at the final name. “Motorcycle owner...”

“Check.”

“Prior assault record against women.”

“Check.”

“Lives within driving distance of the crime scenes.”

“Also check.”

Dakota stared at the name and the subsequent file that opened as Marcus clicked the hyperlinked text. The webpage buffered briefly, slower than usual due to their hotspot, then opened. “Arrested for assault,” Marcus read, “plus multiple traffic citations for speeding at night. Looks like our guy is a joyrider.”

Dakota frowned. “Nighttime rides? Might be the perfect opportunity to pick up unsuspecting victims.”

“Seems to fit. Think maybe we should have a chat with Mr. Ramsey. I'll drive.”

Dakota frowned, hesitating briefly. Normally, she wasn't so sensitive. But the driving comment... was he simply making an offer to be courteous? Was he trying to take charge? Or was he making a subtle jab at her reliability behind a wheel?

Her head still pounded, the darkness had now closed in, surrounding her. All that kept her swimming above gray waters was the hope of catching this bastard before Ms. Lopez went the same way as the rest.

Everything else was a distraction. The killer kept his previous victim for forty-eight hours. Alison Beswick for only twenty-four... What if he was escalating? What if they had even less time to find Ms. Lopez before she suffered the same fate as all the rest.

Dakota knew one thing for sure—her conscience couldn't take another body.

She leaned back, deciding not to mention Marcus's comment as he pulled hurriedly from the parking lot and took to the street. Mr. Ramsey wouldn't likely be home during the day, so she wasn't surprised to watch as Marcus programmed the suspect's last known place of business into the GPS. She let out a faint sigh, eyes half closed as Marcus followed the chirped instructions of the GPS.

CHAPTER THIRTEEN

Arriving at destination on left... The GPS provided its final directive, and Dakota's hand was already darting to the door handle as they pulled into a much nicer parking lot, with freshly painted lines and smooth blacktop, outside a dentist's office.

"He works here?" she muttered, eyes narrowed.

"That's what his file says," Clement replied.

The two of them slipped from their vehicle, shutting the doors with twin motions. No gravel crunched, as there were no stray stones on the fresh blacktop. Similarly, the glass door leading to *Ramsey and Salinas's Dental Practice* was completely clear as if freshly washed. As Dakota pushed the door open, she was confronted by a faint but pleasant odor of lemons. The citrus scent seemed to be coming from a wood-wick candle sputtering on a receptionist's desk. A few children's toys, including a three-dimension wire and wood block puzzle sat in one corner of the waiting room.

The receptionist was smiling politely as the two agents drew near, her hands resting on the counter. Her features were wrinkled, but her eyes bright and alert, streaked with only the lightest touch of mascara.

"Hello dears," she said, flashing a perfect pearly-white. "Do you two have an appointment?"

Marcus returned his own million dollar smile, while Dakota flashed her print-out ID. "FBI," she said, trying to keep her expression neutral. "We need to speak with Demar Ramsey. Is he in?"

"Dr. Ramsey? Umm—y-yes... What is this about?"

"Hang on," Dakota said. "*Doctor*?"

The woman behind the counter looked flustered now, twisting her hands and fidgeting in her seat. "I—I'm sorry, what is this all about? Dr. Ramsey is in the middle of a procedure."

But Dakota was no longer listening. She pointed towards a glass door behind reception, raising an eyebrow as if to say *this way?* And then without awaiting an answer she shoved on through. Time was of the essence. Ms. Lopez couldn't wait until the end of a procedure.

The receptionist's protests fell on deaf ears as Dakota pushed through the swinging glass door, emerged in a small hall and spotted shadows moving under the second door on the left. She made a beeline towards this space, her scowl deep as she stomped forward. Things felt fuzzy, but her focus zeroed in as she shoved the door open, frowning into the space.

The shadows she'd spotted earlier went still across the floor. A handsome, dark man in a white lab coat whirled around, holding a small flashlight in one gloved hand. He wore a face shield, protecting his features from spittle.

An old woman with creased features and silver hair lay unconscious in the chair in front of him, her eyes shut, her mouth half open, kept ajar by a suction tube for spittle.

The woman didn't budge, her head still lolling. But the dentist, Dr. Demar Ramsey was stuttering, wide eyed, holding his flashlight like a shield.

"Lower that!" Dakota demanded, pointing towards the LED.

With trembling fingers, the man tipped the light down. He stuttered, swallowed, tried to speak again but failed.

"Agent Clement, Agent Steele," Marcus called over Dakota's shoulder, frowning into the room. "Are you Dr. Ramsey?"

"I—I am. I'm sorry, did you say *agent*?"

Dakota nodded, then winced again as the LED light flashed towards her eyes once more. "Sir!" she insisted, pointing once more and taking a step nearer to cut him off from an escape route through the side door.

He winced and dropped the penlight as if he'd been scalded. It rolled across the ground, disappearing beneath the dentist's chair and its unconscious occupant.

Any concern she'd had that he might bolt melted quickly as he jutted his hands up and began stammering apologies and explanations before she'd even reached for her cuffs.

"S-sorry," he was saying, shaking his head wildly. "Just a misunderstanding. I—I know that it probably isn't regulation but—well, you can't blame a man for—it was just on the side, you know?"

Dakota gripped the man's shoulder, her fingers grazing the smooth fabric of his white coat as she tried to guide him away from his unconscious patient. "Is there someone who can take care of her?" Dakota demanded.

"I—Umm, Flores is a nurse by training. Just—well—did she let you pass?"

"Flores is the receptionist?"

"Mhmm. Look—I can explain. Really there's no reason for any of this."

They were now back in the hall, and Dakota watched as Marcus went to fetch the receptionist to help with the patient. Dakota affixed a frown as she studied Dr. Ramsey.

"Explain what?" Dakota said, wondering if the man was going to try and minimize the charges and, in so doing, admit to them.

"All of it!" he exclaimed, desperately, his head bumping against the wallpaper. "It was all an accident!"

"Killing those women was accidental? Likely."

He looked like he'd been punched. He wheezed suddenly, and his fingers moved, scrambling for his pocket. Dakota reached to restrain him, but with practiced speed he yanked a small inhaler from his hip and placed it to his lips, taking a long puff.

This man was clean-cut, doe-eyed, fidgeting uncomfortably. Where she gripped his shoulder, he had tensed, and occasionally she caught a mean-eyed glance in her direction. But for the most part, he didn't strike her as the biker-gang sort. Upper crust, educated, professional. This wasn't the sort of person she'd been expecting when reading Demar Ramsey's file.

"You *are* Demar Ramsey, yes?" she said.

Again, his eyes flashed at the question, as if he resented being asked. Or perhaps he resented being asked by *her.*

"Yes!" he said, some temper showing now. "But what do you mean *Killed?* I didn't—did my ex-wife put you up to this? That bitch; she did, didn't she?"

Suddenly, his stammering, docile demeanor switched, and his eyes were blazing now. Marcus had rejoined them in the hall and the receptionist, with a squeak and an askance glance, hurried towards the room with the unconscious patient. Ramsey determinedly looked away from his employee as she passed.

"We don't know anything about your ex-wife," Dakota said sternly. "Was she the victim of the domestic assault? We've seen your record, Mr. Ramsey."

"Doctor! Dr. Ramsey! It wasn't an assault. She started it but hired a better lawyer. That's all! I don't know anything about...," he dropped his voice to a whisper, licked his lips and glanced towards the door, "about *killing.*"

"What were you just admitting to?" Dakota said. "You didn't seem surprised to see us." She studied him, her own expression impassive, doing her best to try and place his emotions.

He stammered again, shaking his head briefly. Then, still whispering, hissing spittle through his clenched teeth he said, "I thought you were here about some of those prescriptions. Like I said, it was all a big accident. A mistake, really."

"What prescriptions?"

He hissed again, trying to cross his arms, which still weren't cuffed, and glaring. "Just a few painkillers," he spat. "My clients need them. Sometimes they have friends who are too intimidated or simply can't afford health insurance. I'm doing them a favor. It's charitable work!"

Dakota blinked. She could feel Marcus's attention shift towards her but just as quickly return to their suspect. *Painkillers.* He thought they were there about *painkillers*? Impossible... He was joking—he had to be... Didn't he?

She shivered and bit her lip. "You've been illegally selling painkillers?"

"Charitably!" He retorted. "What's this about dead women?" He shot a nervous look towards the shut door to his doctor's office.

Dakota said, "You own a motorcycle though, don't you?"

"A—wait what?"

"Just answer the question."

"You own a motorbike."

"No, I don't in fact," he declared, pushing out his chin belligerently. "I used to, but I sold it three weeks ago. To a friend, so we haven't transferred the title yet. It's been busy."

"You *don't* own a motorcycle?"

"It was getting me into trouble," he said, switching to a wheedling tone. "Too many late nights and speeding tickets. No—I got rid of that bike like I got rid of that bitch ex of mine. They were a package deal."

Dakota let out a shaky sigh. "Do you have someone we can verify this with? Who did you sell the motorcycle to?"

"Don Cochran!" he retorted. "Here—here, I'll give you his number now. He'll vouch. I didn't do anything wrong!"

Dakota didn't deny this, nor did she affirm it. She simply shot a confused look towards Marcus who was pulling out his phone. The big man cleared his throat. "Contact info for Mr. Cochran, please. Also, we need to know your whereabouts over the last week. Can you account for Tuesday night? Sunday? Between 10:00 pm and 2:00 am."

"Yes! Yes, I can! Tuesday, at least." he cleared his throat and blushed. "I have AA on Tuesdays. I'm not proud of it—but I'm trying to turn over a new leaf. It's why I sold the bike. My sponsor saw me there.

He can vouch too!"

"Give us his name as well," Dakota interjected, feeling a weight in her stomach. She felt guilty over the thought of arresting a man who sold painkillers on the side, especially given her own problem with drinking. She tried to ignore the AA comment as well.

She shifted uncomfortably, waiting for Marcus to log the contact information. Dr. Ramsey's fingers trembled as he withdrew his own phone.

She didn't listen too carefully, though. Two names—two alibis. They'd check that neither man had gang affiliations of their own. But Ramsey was a damn dentist, not a biker thug. He seemed genuine. She wasn't a betting woman—her vices came in different packages—but if she had been, she would have put all her chips on Ramsey not being their guy.

Another dead end then. So who had taken Ms. Lopez? More importantly—was she even still alive?

CHAPTER FOURTEEN

Miranda Lopez's arms strained above her head, her skull splitting with a thundering headache. She blinked blearily, trying to gather her wits about her, surveying her surroundings as she steadily roused. The pain from her head lanced down her spine, and her heart hammered rapidly. Her lips felt numb and dry.

It was all a blur. As she blinked, adjusting to the faint light glinting through the boarded walls, she tried to think back...

Where was... how had...

And then it all came rushing back with a stomach-curdling spurt of horror. Her eyes widened in terror, and she began to move. But her arms protested the motion, her sockets straining, her wrists sore and stretched in pain.

It took her a second to realize her hands were bound above her.

And now the memories came surging back even faster. She remembered the way the bastard had gripped her arms, locking her in place as he'd sped through the night. Remembered the grumble and roar of the motorcycle engine beneath her desperately tensed legs.

Remembered his gloved hand gripping her, holding her in place.

She wanted to scream now, but the sound was lost in a dry and rasping throat.

He'd hit her over the head. She remembered now. As he'd pulled up a long, disheveled road, past a mailbox stand with no box, she'd tried to break free, to throw herself to the side of the road.

The bike had toppled. She'd hit the ground hard. And then he'd hit her with equal force until she'd stopped moving.

And now...

Now she was here.

Wherever *here* was.

She groaned, trying to wet her lips with a dry tongue, and trying to catch her bearings as her vision slowly cleared.

The sunlight drifted through slits in wooden paneling over large windows. The air smelled of grease and motor oil. The road they'd taken, when she'd tried to escape, had led down an isolated portion of terrain towards an empty house. But this didn't have the appearance of a house. More like a garage, converted into some sort of mechanic's shop. Half-built motorcycles and mechanical parts she had no name for littered dusty workbenches and metal tables.

Two thick metal barrels situated against a corrugated metal wall. The sliding door to the garage?

She groaned again, swinging slowly as she realized her feet were dangling inches above the ground, her arms still stretched above.

"H-help...," she tried to moan, her voice pained. "P—please!" she tried, finding some volume.

She waited, listening. Only the faintest whistle of wind in the distance, and the choking, oppressive weight of sheer, desert silence.

"H-help me, ple—" she began to speak again, but just then a side door was kicked open.

She clapped her lips shut, going suddenly still, trembling and silent. A hunched figure moved into the room now, limping heavily and favoring his right side. The man was wearing the same biker leathers from the night before. The same helmet.

As she stared, terror in her chest, the man slowly reached up, unclasping something beneath his chin and then pulling the helmet.

And then she saw his face.

This, she knew from tv shows, was not a good sign. A kidnapper who showed his face wasn't likely to let her leave and tell anyone about what she'd seen. Her stomach twisted further, terror still wriggling in her gut like burrowing maggots.

She stared at the horrible visage of her captor.

The man had long, dark hair like a stallion. It framed his face, and, in part, seemed intent on obscuring it. He reached up with one black-gloved hand, curling his bangs back behind a damaged ear. In fact, the entire right side of his face was twisted in scars. Burn marks along his chin, his ear, over his eye. The eye was milky-white, like melted plastic.

As he lowered his dark helmet onto one of the desks, she heard the man inhale. A shaky, puffing breath, his single white-eye unblinking as he turned to watch her, studying where she dangled.

The stark terror prickling along her spine nearly held her tongue. But Miranda Lopez hadn't made it this far in life by quaking in the face of adversity. Besides, she could still picture her husband's face in her mind. Thought of her son...

No... she had to try—anything. Something. She had to get out of here.

"P-please," she began, a moan to her voice. "Sir—*please*! Please let me go. I know you didn't mean it. I know this is all a mistake. I won't tell anyone." She paused, swallowing to try and wet her dry throat.

He just continued staring at her, one hand resting against the dome of his motorcycle helmet.

"I have a family! A two-year-old boy. I have... I didn't do anything to you. Why---what do you want?"

She shook horribly, wishing now that she hadn't asked such a fateful question. Did she really want to know what this man *wanted?* She saw pain in his eyes. Pain and a type of hatred. She'd seen that look before. Growing up in the home she had, things had been violent, dangerous. She'd been fortunate to get out when she did.

Her career had protected them. Her salary, her status had brought them into a safe neighborhood. Had made powerful friends.

But now none of that mattered. She wished she'd turned down the business trip. Wished she'd spent the night in their lovely, two-story home, snuggled by the fireplace beneath that thick, quilted blanket.

The man remained standing behind the workbench, his fingers still lingering on the helmet, stroking it in an odd, almost erotic way. His other hand moved to the table and slowly picked up a pair of pliers. He examined the tool, tilting his head curiously and inhaling once more, emitting that same, rasping, painful sound.

The edge of the pliers was stained in a dark liquid, and Miranda's eyes bugged, sweat dripping down the side of her face.

"You want mercy?" her asked in that horrible, rasping voice. It sounded as if his words were course, like sandpaper. "You ask for mercy?" he repeated, swallowing loudly.

"P-please," she moaned. "Just let me go. I won't tell anyone."

"Liar," he said laconically, with a smirk. "You would tell." He tapped a finger to the uninjured side of his nose. "Now let me tell you something..." He took a step towards her, pliers still gripped in one hand. He limped heavily, dragging his leg behind him as he approached. "You showed me no mercy," he said, whispering now as if it pained him to speak at full volume for too long. "Do you remember?"

She stared blankly at him, trying to understand his words. "I—I what?"

"You offered no mercy when you gave me this." He lifted the stained pliers, dragging them across his bumpy, scarred skin, and letting out a sound like a snake's hiss. He winced, limped once more and was now standing a few paces away from her. He examined her up and down as if she were a slab of beef in a butcher's shop, his single good eye lingering, then flicking towards her face.

"You've caused me two decades of pain," he whispered. "Twenty years is a long time to suffer. I'll be far more merciful to you than you ever were to me."

"I—I think you've mistaken me for someone. I've never met you before. I don't know you!"

He grinned now, flashing teeth. "That's how it always starts with you, doesn't it? Ask me to kill you. Hmm? That's the way out. Tell me to kill you and I will. Would you like me to?"

She stared in horror, her pulse racing as he slowly lowered the pliers from his cheek and used them to brush more perfectly conditioned and shampooed hair out of his face.

"N—no! Please let me go!" she pleaded.

"You will ask me to soon enough. You always do."

"I—I don't know you, sir, p-p-please. Please I have a child."

"I was your child!" He screamed now, spittle gushing from his mouth. He coughed though, bending double for a moment and holding a hand to his throat. His shoulders shook as pain racked his body and he tried to stand upright.

"You shouldn't have invited him into our home," he whispered in that hoarse voice. "Shouldn't have left me with him. It's your fault this is happening, Mother. It always has been. And if I find you again tonight, I'll have to dispose of this one here..."

He was ranting now, raving, waving the pliers about and finally jutting them towards her in a flourish.

She just stared in stunned silence, her heart hammering so loudly she thought she might collapse if not for the ropes securing her to the ceiling.

"The last time I had you here... You wailed and screamed so loudly your throat sounded like mine." He giggled, nodding his head at his own words as if somehow agreeing with his assessment. "Scream. Go on. Do it!"

"P-please."

"SCREAM!"

"HELP!" She screeched, kicking out to try to keep him away. "PLEASE! PLEASE SOMEONE HELP ME!"

He laughed now, howling along with her at the ceiling, his arms at his side, screeching like a wolf at night. As he howled, she pleaded into the air, pleaded desperately.

But he was just grinning, laughing at her screams, almost as if he enjoyed them. He thought she was someone else. Someone he knew. She'd never met the man before—he was clearly insane. But none of that mattered now. All that mattered was what the unbound man with the pliers thought.

He suddenly darted forward, his rough skin scraping against her smooth cheek. She shuddered in revulsion as he pressed near her, his lips tickling her ear. "Listen," he whispered, the hiss itching her ear canal. "Please kill me... That's all you have to say, understand? I'll be merciful. I'll do it. But until then..."

He clicked his tongue and made a kissing sound. "Things will go badly."

Then he howled in her ear, laughing louder as she kicked and tried to scream, desperately thrashing, determined to live. Determined to see her husband and child once more. It couldn't end like this.

She refused.

But what could she possibly do about it?

CHAPTER FIFTEEN

Another dead end. Dakota was getting sick of these. Back at the hotel, she sat on the edge of her bed, her laptop open next to her. The small glass bottles had been tidied and put in the recycling bin. Her suitcase was neat, angled parallel to the wall. Everything about the room was properly arranged. Even the bathroom curtains were symmetrical now.

Dakota liked cleaning things, liked organizing. It gave her a sense of control that she so sorely lacked in other areas. Now, though, her fingers tensed against the keyboard. She didn't blink as she scanned the information on the buzzing screen.

Back to square one. Dr. Ramsey's alibis had *both* checked out. He wasn't their guy. Someone else was out there hunting women. Someone else had Miranda Lopez in their grasp.

She was back in the FBI database, scanning the longer list of names before they'd pruned it too much. Motorcycle owners with violent records. But how else could she narrow it? They didn't have time to chase every possibility. More importantly, Ms. Lopez didn't have the time.

She glanced towards her door which was still cracked. She could hear Marcus's voice echoing from the hall where he was still on the line double-checking Ramsey's alibis. It didn't matter, though—he'd been telling the truth. Dr. Ramsey didn't read like a serial killer. A bit of a sociopath, perhaps, but not a killer.

She stared at the database, frowning at the small, white search bars on the side... One of the bars wanted information about the make and model of the bike. But no witnesses had actually seen it. It would be good if they knew what *kind* of motorcycle they were looking for, but there was no such luck. In Nevada, most of the bikes made a racket.

That was all witnesses near the crime scenes attested to; they'd heard the sound of a motorcycle fleeing the spot before the bodies had been discovered.

Dakota hesitated briefly, her brow wrinkling...

They had *heard*... But no one had *seen* anything.

"Huh," she muttered to herself.

What if it wasn't a motorcycle? What if it only *sounded* like one? Dirt-bikes wouldn't appear in the same registry. Nor would ATVs. Or, hell, snowmobiles and the like. Other engines could be mistaken for some type of motorcycle.

She adjusted the search parameters, clicked enter and waited.

More names appeared on the list. Once more, she narrowed the results by geography and victim type. Two of the names were still in prison. One had moved out of state. But that left three names remaining.

She frowned. One of them owned an ATV. Two of them owned dirt-bikes. She clicked on the first name and just as quickly clicked away, wrinkling her nose. His victims were underage. Not the profile.

She clicked to another of the two remaining names. One of the men had been in and out of juvie most of his life. He'd gotten into an altercation at a bar where he'd accidentally, according to witnesses, elbowed a woman. She'd pressed charges.

Dakota frowned. This didn't fit the profile either.

She moved to the last name. She would keep the accidental elbower on the list just in case, but as she scanned the final name, she knew this was who she needed to prioritize.

A competitive, off-road dirt bike racer. His file included a list of his accolades. Burt Riggs, thirty-three years of age. On his way to becoming a champion in his field according to a couple of links to online articles. Recently, though, he'd been ejected from the league for punching a female fan that had taunted him.

He'd lost everything in one swing and had only finished his sentence a few weeks ago. He lived twenty miles from where the first body had been found...

She whistled faintly. "Hello there..."

The female victim of the assault was in her twenties.

"Marcus!" she called towards the door. "I think I found something."

The voice faded in the hall, and the door slowly opened. The big man raised an eyebrow, peering in at her curiously.

Dakota was already scanning the file for an address. "Burt Riggs," she said. "Just recently got out on an assault beef. You can drive!"

She shoved off the bed, memorized the address then closed the laptop, hastily stowing it back in her satchel. She took care to tuck the wired charger neatly in the Velcro strap. Once everything was pretty and placed, she zipped it up, shouldered the bag and marched toward the door. She swallowed, absentmindedly touching her fingers to her turtleneck. "You good to go?"

Marcus shrugged. “If you say I need to, yah. Who is Cinderella? And what's the glass slipper?”

“I'll tell you on the way.”

***

“Lovely,” Dakota said, wrinkling her nose as they pulled to a crunching halt on a dirt road, facing a crowded trailer park.

One of the trailers settled on what might have been termed a double lot, the walls faded, the stacks of tires outside nearly reaching the underside of the greasy, gray windows. A few lights were on in neighboring vehicles, and an old couple sat on a makeshift porch, beneath a green umbrella further down the road. The older couple sipped on glasses with brown liquid and clinking ice cubes and sat in front of a much tidier, well-kept trailer.

Dakota gave a little wave of greeting, which the neighbors returned jovially, before returning her attention to the trailer in question.

“You're sure this is it?” Marcus asked, one hand holding his passenger-side door open.

Dakota sighed but gave a quick nod. “That's what his license says. This is it.”

The two of them pushed out of their borrowed vehicle and took to the dusty, dirt road, stepping carefully onto the flat, cracked asphalt drive leading to the front door of the worn-down trailer.

Marcus rubbed at his chin, taking a quick step to the side and peering along behind the trailer, towards a second row of homes which faced in the other direction towards a street that curled like a 'U'.

“Guess Mr. Riggs needs to be mobile to travel for his races,” Dakota murmured softly, peering at the place.

Agent Clement frowned. “Thought you said he was banned from competitions.”

“Yeah. Doesn't look like he landed on his feet either,” she murmured, staring at the home with a mild look of disgust. The tires were slashed, the walls stained yellow. A small, neon sign in the window flashed the word *Riggs* in pink, strobing lights.

Beer cans and liquor bottles littered the front door, next to a toppled, silver trash can filled with similar debris.

Dakota stared at the empty bottles, the faint brown stains on the dusty ground near the lips of the dispensaries. She shifted uncomfortably, one hand hovering, extended towards the door handle.

"You good?" Marcus said.

"Fine—Yes, just fine." She turned the handle, pulling the door open and stepping back as a blast of foul wind caught her. She wrinkled her nose, waving a hand in front of her face before calling into the dark, unlit trailer. "Mr. Riggs? Hello? FBI!"

She heard a burp then the sound of smashed glass. A second later, her eyes adjusted to the dark confines of the ill-kept place.

Burt Riggs reclined on a couch, more bottles scattered around him. He looked as if he hadn't shaved in a week, and he smelled as if he hadn't showered in twice as long. He blinked blearily up at them, clearly half-drunk, moaning at the sudden invasion of light.

"Geross!" he called, jumbling his words incoherently.

"Burt Riggs," Dakota said, her voice steely. "We need to speak with you, sir."

The man tried to shift but sent a bottle tumbling from his chest. He nearly fell off the couch, onto shattered glass, but at the last minute caught himself and grunted, hefting his weight as he turned away from the door, trying to shield his face from the light.

Marcus stood just behind Dakota, as the small door frame was too small for the two of them. Part of her felt a flash of shame, looking at the man on the couch. Wallowing, half-drunk—was this what she'd looked like when Marcus and Casper had come to confront her back in Rapid City?

She winced in disgust, feeling a hot jet of shame prickle across her cheeks. Her stomach twisted. Was she staring into her future? Her past? Was this what her soul looked like?

The man wiggled, slowly lifting and propping his head up, bending an elbow. "What?" he snapped, still wincing.

She could practically feel the headache from here. Her fingers touched her long sleeves and she said, "Mr. Riggs we need to speak with you about your whereabouts over the last few days."

"Been here," he snapped. "Now get out."

Dakota shook her head. "You need to come with us, sir. Please."

He glared at her from red-ringed eyes, shaking his head firmly. "Like hell I will. Already lost everything. Now cops hassling me? Don't think so. Get out of my house."

Dakota sighed. She shot Marcus a look. But before he could step past her to intervene, she took a couple of quick steps into the trailer, reaching for Mr. Riggs. "Sir, you need to come with us. This isn't a debate. It's important you answer some questions. For your sake and ours." *And Ms. Lopez,* she thought to herself.

Burt Riggs wasn't hearing it, though. He ripped his hand from hers, slapping at her knuckles. "Get lost!" he bellowed. "Leave me alone! I didn't do shit!" He tried to kick at her suddenly and Dakota slipped the blow, moving her hips. She caught his leg, then tilted it, lifting him as if with a fulcrum.

He bellowed then kicked out with his other foot. Now his blow landed, catching Dakota's arm. She shoved at his leg, twisting him on the couch and ducked in, head angled to avoid catching an elbow. She also twisted *around* the couch, flinging herself over it in one quick motion and putting her forearm beneath the man's neck.

"Sir! Calm down!" she said firmly. She didn't squeeze. Not yet. But she had him in the beginnings of a rear naked choke.

Mr. Riggs, though, was growing even more agitated. With a howl, he tried to rip at her fingers, but she'd already tucked those beneath her other arm. So instead, he gasped, spittle flecking her sleeve and then chomped down *hard.*

His teeth dug into her arm, and Dakota's eyes bulged. She yelped, yanking her arm back in pain.

"Get off!" he screamed, gasping and lunging now. He didn't go towards the door, where Marcus was still standing, but instead bolted straight towards the nearest window. It was open, allowing the faintest of breezes to flutter through.

"Clement!" Dakota bellowed, still hissing and grasping at her bit arm. "Grab him!"

She was already moving too, hurtling the couch and lunging after the half-drunk man, but he was busy shimmying through the window. Marcus had taken a step into the trailer, realized he wouldn't reach the man in time and instead cursed, rushing back out the door in hot pursuit.

Dakota grabbed a shoe, but the man kicked free. Now, holding an old, stinky sneaker, she stared as Burt Riggs slipped through the window and tumbled out the side of the trailer. A sound like a *thump* proceeded a long groan. But then a grunt and tottering footsteps.

"Stop!" Dakota yelled. She winced again as she rubbed her arm. She hoped she didn't have to get a tetanus shot for this nonsense. "Mr. Riggs—stop right there!"

But her voice was drowned out by a sudden, chugging growl. Marcus, who was outside the house cursed. A second later, Dakota heard the growl of the engine. She flung herself towards the window, hands splayed on either side and stared, bug-eyed, as Burt Riggs ripped from behind the trailer house, sitting astride a dirt bike.

He flashed the middle-finger as he veered around Marcus, spitting up a cloud of dust. Clement tried to grab the dirt-bike champ but missed, stumbling to the ground in his zeal.

Dakota only had a second to react. Already, Riggs was picking up speed, hastening towards the main road. In seconds, he'd be gone.

Clearly, he was more attentive than he'd been letting on. Was it all just an act? Had he been playing them?

Dakota winced again at the bite on her arm. She scowled after the fleeing motorcycle, then reached a decision. No way to catch him. Only one chance.

She pulled her weapon from the holster, feeling the smooth, weighty heft of the handgun. It had been a while since she'd wielded this thing.

Now she raised it, aimed through the window, shoulders squared.

She took a second longer, making sure she wouldn't accidentally hit Riggs himself.

Then, she squeezed the trigger.

The gunshot rang in her ears but was nearly instantly drowned out by the bursting tire. The back wheel exploded, and the bike suddenly swerved.

Riggs let out a shout as his bike flipped with him on it.

He cursed as he went head over heels and seconds later the machine landed with him in a whirring, groaning, sputtering heap on the dusty road.

Marcus blinked, staring at the wreck. He turned slowly, looking at where Dakota leaned out the window. "W-wow," he muttered. "Umm..." He glanced at the weapon in her hand, then swallowed. It said a lot that Marcus Clement, of all people, was at a loss for words.

Dakota winced, ducking back through the window and hastily holstering her weapon. Technically, she wasn't an agent. She'd quit. As an acting agent, a consultant, Marcus had gone to bat for her. A bad shooting would reflect on him as well as her.

She'd hit the tire, but judging by the groaning sounds from Riggs, he'd still suffered.

She hurried out the trailer door, grateful to draw in fresh air once again. Marcus was already jogging towards the fallen biker. Clement's phone was clutched in his massive hand, and even from where she rushed forward, by the trailer, Dakota could hear barked instructions. "Paramedics!" Marcus was saying. "Looks like a broken leg—yeh, hurry. Sending the address now."

Dakota winced, jogging forward towards where Burt Riggs was mewling and hollering something fierce, his hands clutching past his bike towards his leg which was pinned beneath the machine.

Marcus Clement let out a faint whistle, then in a louder voice called, "Are you alright?"

"Hello no!" Riggs screamed. "My damn leg! Gah! Get this thing off!"

Marcus nodded quickly, reached down with one hand and—in a herculean show of strength—casually lifted the bike, toppling it off to the other side of the road.

Burt Riggs moaned, collapsing back, arms and legs splayed as he stared dazedly at the sky.

"Damn it," he muttered beneath his breath.

"Shouldn't have bitten her," Marcus muttered beneath his breath as Dakota neared. "She tends to escalate things quickly. She doesn't start fights, but she ends them."

"My leg man! Is it still there? Dear God—it's not gone, is it?"

"Your leg is fine," Marcus said quickly. "Looks like a break. You'll be hobbling around in no time. Sit still. Paramedics are coming."

Dakota stood a pace away, out of Riggs's line of sight. She looked towards Marcus and mouthed, "Sorry."

The big man gave a quick nod, but his smile seemed somewhat forced. She stared towards the blasted tire—the rubber ripped to shreds. She also stared at the bike. A small, compact machine. The seat was narrow, the thing outfitted in such a way to shed as much weight as possible while maintaining speed.

She let out a shaking little breath. In the distance, she thought she heard sirens rapidly approaching.

CHAPTER SIXTEEN

Dakota was grateful Marcus hadn't brought up the shooting. Hardly an orthodox move to go for a motorcycle wheel. Then again, she hadn't been intending to hurt the man, only halt him. Now, though, there lay evidence of the best laid plans...

Burt Riggs reclined on a hospital bed, one of his legs elevated and in a cast. One arm was handcuffed to the cot's rail while the other gripped the television remote like a medieval mace, brandishing it at the two of them.

Dakota had allowed Marcus to take the lead on this one. For one, he'd always had a better bedside manner than she did. But also, Riggs had surmised the source of the gunshot and spent half the interrogation shooting angry glances in her direction.

Dakota busied herself pretending like she was examining one of the electronic machines next to the bed while simultaneously listening open-eared to Riggs's responses.

"Don't know anythin' about no girls," he was saying, scowling at Dakota, scowling at Marcus's questions and scowling in general.

"No one was with you those nights?" Marcus pressed, rounding about to the same line of questioning from earlier but also trying to fish for new information.

"Shit—I told you, didn't I? Black out. Wasted. Gone. Bugged out. I wasn't in no state to be nowhere but my trailer."

"Alone," Marcus said carefully.

"Damn right. You making something of it?"

"No sir," Marcus replied patiently. "It's only helpful to *verify* an alibi if others were around."

"Psh. Ask the pizza delivery driver. He'd know. Ordered from him twice on Tuesday. Twice more Monday. Also... Yeah, buncha times. Got this sick new app, man. I get points for every order."

Marcus sighed, massaging his nose. "I'm going to need the information of the restaurant you ordered from."

Riggs just groaned, pressing his head back into the pillow. "Man, can't this wait? My leg is killing me. Imma sue—you bet your ass I will."

Marcus frowned. "Correct me if I'm wrong but driving under the influence is a violation of your parole."

The man blinked, then looked stunned as if he'd been slapped. "Y—you wouldn't dare," he said.

Marcus just shrugged. Dakota shifted uncomfortably. She knew her partner was going to bat on her behalf, but that didn't mean she had to like it. The last thing she needed was an investigation into a shooting. As an acting agent, she was allowed to carry her weapon, on a temporary basis, but the regulations for suspension or legal action were much lower in her position.

Besides, the more trouble she caused, the more likely Marcus suffered for it. Being her partner for nearly a decade had caused him enough trouble. She didn't want to pile on any further.

As she listened to Riggs, though, she let out a faint sigh. It would be easy enough to check with a delivery driver. If Riggs really was wasted at the time of the kidnappings and murders, it would be unlikely he'd had the mental capacity to pull any of this off with such anonymity. Even if he'd been faking... looking at him now, at the state of his place—some things *couldn't* be faked in the face of the stark demands of reality.

Besides, she already had her own doubts. She thought back to the small motorcycle seat she'd seen. A dirt bike in her mind was a larger machine. The one Riggs rode was tiny. Built for speed and competition no doubt.

The problem, though, with a tiny machine was that it had no space to place a body. The women, when kidnapped, had to be put *somewhere*. But the seat alone, when she'd examined it back at the trailer park, had barely been large enough for Riggs himself. Certainly, there was no space for two people.

Dakota sighed, turning away towards the door as Marcus jotted down the information of the pizza restaurant Riggs claimed as his alibi.

It would check out. The bike was too small. The man too sloppy. This wasn't a killer; he was a wreck.

Dakota winced at the characterization, wondering if others thought similarly of her. Vaguely, the voices continued to drone behind her. They were quickly approaching evening. Which meant Dakota had gone far too long without a drink of her own. But after seeing Riggs's place, his appearance... She felt another lance of shame and disgust.

Why did she have to be like this? Why the hell couldn't she just *change*?

Just then, her phone began to ring.

Dakota hesitated, fingers hovering. For a wild moment she wanted nothing more than to chuck the device across the room and retreat. To return home, to hide in Rapid City, in her dark, small apartment. She missed the solitude. Missed the quiet.

But didn't miss the loneliness...

The phone continued to ring.

Hesitantly, feeling a rising sense of anxiety, she pulled the device and checked the number. It didn't display. There was no message about the caller ID being blocked, or it being a hidden number. Rather, it was simply blank. She stared, wetting her lips. The last time she'd received a call from a no-name, no icon number had been three months ago.

FBI. Not just the FBI, but supervising agents. Who was currently heading up Clement's division? After the incident three months ago, a couple of their bosses had been "moved laterally." Which was just bureaucratic talk for getting axed slowly while trying to keep lawsuits or pension cuts at a minimum.

She waited a second, half hoping the phone would go quiet, but it kept ringing insistently. At last, with a grimace she answered, but kept her tone polite as ever.

"Hello?" she murmured.

"Dakota Steele?" A voice replied.

A croaking, well-articulated voice, like that of an English professor past her prime. "Umm, yes... Agent..."

"Supervising Agent Carter," the voice said stiffly. "I don't believe we've met."

"Right, right—I heard of you. You, umm... you replaced—"

"I did," Carter said curtly. "We can reminisce later, but I need to speak to you about your field assignment with Agent Clement." Dakota could practically hear the pursed lips over the phone.

"O—oh?"

"I was opposed to his request," she said without hesitation. "And this is why—is it true you shot at a fleeing suspect?"

"No—I mean, I shot at his dirt bike. Not at him."

A long, no-nonsense sigh. "Is he currently in the hospital?"

"Yes."

"And was it directly due to actions you took involving your firearm?"

"I—yes." Dakota stood in the doorway, the phone glued to her cheek, wondering if there was some way she could backtrack, or help

Agent Carter see it from her point of view. But why? Dakota didn't care if the woman disapproved of her. She had no intention of returning to the BAU. This was a one-off. She'd done it to get Casper off her back, to help Marcus out.

On the other hand, she didn't want to leave Marcus up shit creek with no paddle. So she said, "Agent Clement was completely clear of the scene. He instantly called paramedics and tended to the suspect."

"I see. And yet half an hour ago, Agent Clement was telling me *he* gave the order for the shot."

"He's probably mistaken," she blurted out. "He's just covering for me."

She was now in the hall and shot a quick look back towards where Clement was still interviewing Mr. Riggs. Her heart pulsed with gratitude that Marcus would go to bat for her like that. But on the other hand, she didn't want to ruin his career further.

Their last case had implications on his prospects for advancement. He didn't bring it up, but she knew she'd already done enough to damage his reputation. She heard a pause on the phone, then blinked, realizing she hadn't been paying attention.

"I'm sorry, what was that?"

"Ms. Steele," the supervisor said, her tone crisp, "I told Agent Clement this was a bad idea when he proposed it. He insisted. What little social capital he has remaining here is quickly deteriorating. Understand? Any more mishaps and I'm pulling *both* of you off the case. Do I make myself clear?"

"Marcus didn't do—"

"Do I *make myself clear?*"

Dakota bit her lip. She inhaled shakily, calming a sudden spurt of temper. Fighters could often be hotheads, but under a trainer like Casper Little, she'd learned to fight her own pride. Authority figures didn't bother her. Even now, getting chewed out, she knew Agent Carter was trying to do what was best. But if this reflected on Marcus at all, she'd never be able to forgive herself.

"Alright," she said quickly. "Clear. Nose clean, eyes bright. You won't have any more trouble."

"Good," Carter snapped. Then hung up.

Dakota stood in the hallway outside the hospital room, closing her eyes and inhaling faintly as she tried to calm her riled nerves.

The slow, tangible darkness descended on her again like a woolen blanket. Why had she come here? Why had she been so selfish to think she could do this?

She'd never been a good agent, not really. Despite what Marcus tried to say, she should've stayed in the cage. Like an animal. People who grew up how she did, with the decisions she'd made didn't deserve a second chance, did they?

Her head pulsed. She needed a drink. Needed *something* to help. This was unbearable. And now, as much as she wanted to quit, she couldn't. Not just for Ms. Lopez, but Marcus's career. He was counting on her.

He'd made that mistake before. Fool me once...

But the shame was all on her.

It would all be so much easier to run back to South Dakota, crawl into a bottle and never emerge.

"Dakota!" Marcus called from inside the hospital room. "The delivery driver is working today. Want to be on the call?"

Dakota looked away, not wanting to meet Marcus's kind gaze. "Nah," she said. "I'm going to get a coffee. You want anything?"

She didn't wait to listen for his response. Already, she strode hurriedly up the hospital hall, making a beeline towards the stairs. She took them three at a time, circling down towards the first floor. A nurse got in her way and Dakota side-stepped quickly, as if she was back in the cage, avoiding an opponent's jab. With the same fluid motion, she picked up the pace and rushed through the sliding glass doors.

Damn coffee... Caffeine wasn't what she needed. Because she did *need* it. Without it... She just needed it all to stop. Just a second to think clearly. It helped keep the edge off, didn't it? This time, she'd be doing it for Marcus. That was noble. For Ms. Lopez. A little sip or two to save a life? What could be bad about that?

She stalked up the street, ignoring the parking garage where their loaner sat. She broke into a jog, rounding the wing of the hospital, beelining towards the gas station she'd spotted a mile back. Interesting how a craving mind picked up on certain things.

And this time, Marcus wasn't here to stop her. Feet thumped against pavement, her arms in motion. Despite some of her consumption habits, Dakota was still in good shape. She rolled back her sleeves, indifferent to who spotted the tattoos now. Quicker, faster, she sprinted now, away from the hospital, head down, ignoring the cars passing by and the occasional pedestrians strolling along the sidewalk.

She raced to the edge of the street, turned to peer down the curb towards the gas station. The neon lights displayed the gas prices for the day, and a couple of trucks navigated around each other in the tight corridor between two pumps, jockeying for position.

Her brow slick, her breathing coming quickly, she covered the rest of the distance at a dead sprint, arms pumping like pistons.

And then she reached the glass door, gasping. She didn't hesitate this time. Didn't allow her body the permission. She pushed right on through, marched to the refrigerator, grabbed a cheap pack of beers and dragged it back to the counter. She placed the six pack on the marble, adjusting it carefully to be parallel with the window. As if somehow a tidy counter would make up for this stupid choice.

"Just this," she said curtly.

The man behind the counter hesitated and began to point to a sign about required ID for liquor sales, but she just glared, slammed her card into the reader and waited.

Something in her gaze must have caused the cashier pause. He sighed, muttering something under his breath, but then clicked through the screen on his side of the counter. The card reader began to beep, and she removed her debit, grabbing the sixpack and muttering. "No receipt needed. Thanks."

She turned abruptly on her heel and marched towards the back of the store, making a beeline towards the bathrooms. In one hand, her sixpack. She pushed the bathroom door open with a foot, stepped in, locked it with her sleeve and nearly collapsed on the sink.

The bottles clinked where she dumped them into the porcelain bowl. Her fingers shook badly as she tried to remove the cap to the first drink. She could see herself moving in the reflection but refused to look. Couldn't bear it.

Her fingers continued to shake. She let out a faint whimpering sound but quieted just as quickly. She didn't need the cashier calling the cops. If she took a drink, it would be opening the doors of hell. She wouldn't stop at one. Wouldn't stop at three or six. She knew herself too well for that.

Her hand continued to shake badly. If she did this, if she opened that bottle, she'd be useless to Marcus. Useless to the case. Useless to save Miranda from whatever hellhole she was now being kept in.

Useless.

She let out a shuddering, shaking breath, trying to put up a fight of will. And she battled. For a full minute she stood there as if frozen in time, her flesh screaming, her mind warring with itself.

But what was the damn use?

She twisted the cap with her hand, ignoring the metal ridges pressing into her skin.

CHAPTER SEVENTEEN

Marcus Clement stood outside the hospital room, lowering his phone with a feeling of discontent rising in his stomach. Only partly because the delivery driver had confirmed Riggs's alibi. But mostly because Dakota was gone.

Coffee, she'd said.

He didn't believe her. He knew where she'd gone. He sighed, a long, weary exhalation. He closed his eyes, pulling his spectacles off and gripping them between thumb and forefinger. He lingered in the hall, feeling like a shadow. His heart panged.

He never should have accused Dakota of failure in their last case. Three months was a long time for words to heal, but evidently not long enough. She'd always struggled somewhat with demons from her past, but their last case had only served to exacerbate the issue.

"Oh, Dakota...," he muttered faintly. Part of him wondered if he ought to go looking for her. But he'd already tried to stop her once. It wasn't his place to do it again.

He opened his eyes, peering out the large window into the graying skies. He missed Dakota Steele. Not this version of her—part of her in pain, the other part trying to hide from it. He missed his old partner. She'd been serious, solemn then also, but only in stages. She'd laughed, she'd smiled—not often, but enough. She'd seemed... perhaps not happy, but bordering happiness.

And now... now her eyes just held shame. She'd made mistakes before... *They'd* made mistakes before. It had been a team effort. The two of them hadn't hit on every case. No one could. But at least they'd made their mistakes as a unit. But that last one... they'd fought. They'd argued. They simply couldn't agree. And he knew why. She now knew why. It had seemed so obvious to Marcus, but Dakota had been battling her own demons. And someone had died because of it.

He felt his own eyes misting at the thought of his partner's pain. He'd always been drawn to the hurting, the broken things of the world. Growing up as he had, with two loving parents in an upper middle-class home, he'd had everything provided for him. A car, an education, tuition fees. He'd had more love than he knew what to do with.

He couldn't remember the last time he'd spent a birthday or Christmas alone. Dakota... he didn't think had spent a holiday with anyone else in years. His therapist told him he had a bit of a savior complex, but also a big heart.

He wasn't sure how true this was, but he knew that it wasn't pity that committed him to his partner. He was loyal to her, sure—but it was a reciprocal loyalty. At least, so he'd thought. It had pained him when she'd up and quit. Almost as if she'd abandoned him.

But he also knew her value. She studied people better than most. Her intuition for intention was off the charts. She was waspishly smart, especially in unconventional ways. She also knew better than most how to handle herself in a fight.

They'd failed the last case together, but over the last ten years... Nearly a ninety percent closure rate. Almost unheard of in the department. They'd made an excellent team.

But was he just grasping at straws now? Was it all dead and gone? Was he trying to unearth something best left buried?

Maybe the days of Steele and Clement were over.

Maybe he just had to resign himself to a change in season, to the death of an era...

His brow flickered at the thought, but then his lip twisted in a sneer.

Hell no.

He wasn't ready to give up on her. Not yet.

He'd never forgive himself if he did.

But she sure wasn't interested in listening to his opinion. So he had to pull out all the stops. Collusion—that's what she'd call it. But he'd done the same back in South Dakota. A little bit of collusion had gone a long way then.

He needed a trump card. Needed backup.

And he knew exactly who to call.

Marcus pulled his phone out, cycling to one of his most recently dialed numbers and then raised the phone, waiting patiently, his dark gaze still fixated on the gray horizon.

***

Dakota sat beneath the bathroom sink, breathing shallowly. Her six pack still rested in the basin above her. The single open bottle still in one hand. Her other palm was open, the cap from the beer nestled there.

She didn't care that her shoulders were pressed to the moldered wall beneath the gas-station bathroom sink. Did her best not to look in the direction of the horrible state of the toilet. Promptly ignored the faint knocking on the door as the cashier checked to see if the space was still occupied.

"A minute!" she shouted and returned her attention to the little white promises in her hand. How long had she been down here, staring? Fighting?

A longer fight than any she'd ever faced in the cage... And with no end in sight. She just wanted to tap out.

She wasn't thinking of Marcus anymore. Wasn't thinking of the case. Wasn't thinking of anything.

She raised the bottle, pressing the glass to her lips with an oddly steady hand.

She closed her eyes in deep regret and grief, while at the same time her brain fired off chemical rewards simply for the concession, for giving in. This was only the prelude to the relief. As she began to tip the drink, her phone suddenly began to ring.

She went stiff, flinching and wincing suddenly as her head banged against a curving metal pipe.

"Dammit," she muttered to herself.

The phone continued to ring insistently. This time, she was determined to let it go to voicemail. She didn't need to be chewed out by another supervising agent she didn't know, or, worse, Marcus. He was no dummy—he'd likely figured out where she'd gone.

She reached into her pocket, clicked off the call.

Her phone began to ring again. Almost more insistently, if such a thing were possible.

She growled now, her usual demeanor of calm and control cracking completely. Her eyes bugged in frustration, and she ripped the phone from her pocket, lifting it furiously. "What?" she demanded, spittle flying.

"What yourself!" Came back an equally irritated, but familiar voice.

She winced. "Coach," she muttered.

"Dakota," Casper Little replied.

She sighed. "I can't talk right now."

"You hang up," her old mentor said, "And I'll go to your place and dump garbage all over your bed."

She blinked. "What?"

"You heard me."

"That's not fair."

“No? Well, I never taught you to fight fair. I taught you to win.” The old Irishman was doing nothing to conceal his temper. She blinked against the unrelenting pounding of his words. It took her a second, but then her own anger arose. “Dammit, Coach—I'm not in the mood. I'll call you later.”

“No, you won't. Let me guess, hiding in some alley? A parked car? Not a gas station bathroom again, surely?”

She winced but scowled. She'd already taken a stand and wasn't about to back down. Even if he was right. “What do you want, Coach? I don't have anything to give you.”

“Nah, you don't. Didn't when I took you off the street then either, did you?”

She hesitated, feeling her stomach twist. She didn't want to remember that far back. Didn't want to remember how they'd met. Hell, she'd kicked a couple of hoods' asses when they'd accosted what she'd initially thought was a defenseless old man with a cane. Turned out to be Casper Little. At the time, she'd been going through a rough patch. Had already left home. Her so-called father.

She hadn't had a place to stay. Anywhere or anyone to call her own.

The coach had seen something in her, though. He'd invited her to the gym. Eventually even let her sleep on his couch in his own house.

He'd always treated her fair. Treated her well. Even... even liked her.

As impossible as that was to believe at times.

And now there she sat, like a chastised schoolgirl beneath a bathroom sink, glaring at a toilet with glass pressed to her lips. She might have laughed at the ridiculous image if she hadn't been so embarrassed.

He was telling the truth. Which made it worse. He had taken her off the streets when she'd been a kid. He'd trained her. Treated her as one of his own.

“You always know how to twist the guilt knife,” she said, scowling still.

“I don't give two shits, Tastee!” he retorted. “Now you listen to me—you've never been a quitter before.”

“Did Marcus call you?”

“Who?”

She sighed. “He did. Just leave me alone, Casper...,” she said, trailing off, her voice going numb and aching with pain. “Please...”

“You sound exhausted, Tastee.”

“I've been exhausted.”

“I know that...,” his tone softened a little, and she could picture the wrinkles around his eyes creasing as they so often did when he watched her. He'd always tried to hide his concern, his compassion. He needed to be the 'hard wall.' That's what he called himself. The hard wall off which soft things rebounded.

His coaching style was what had made her tough. Was what had taken a girl off the street, put her through training, nearly made a champion out of her and then seen her through college and to the FBI. Compassion propelled some to hugs and kisses. Compassion in Casper's hand created champions.

So where had it all gone with her?

“I can smell the pity party from here,” he said, his tone hardening again. “Buck up, kid. I know it hurts. I damn well know it hurts. But you're doing nothing for no one by beating yourself up.”

“Sometimes I wish...,” she trailed off, her mind flaring with panic. She refused to voice such thoughts out loud. The pity party. The regret.

“Cut it out!” he said suddenly. “Cut out that thinking. I mean it. You're no victim, Dakota. Don't you doubt it. You aren't a quitter. Never have been. But you damn sure seem to want to act like one.”

Again, she felt like she'd been slapped. But gentle words, soft touches, soothing tones were all well and good. Marcus provided that sort of encouragement aplenty.

Sometimes, a little bit of pain, a little bit of hard truth jolted her.

It didn't help her forget. But... it brought a perspective. One she wasn't sure she wanted to look through.

“Dakota, listen to me,” he said finally, his voice firm. “What happened to that girl three months ago wasn't your fault.”

She flinched suddenly. The hint of beer against her mouth tasting sour all of a sudden.

“Forget about it,” she muttered.

“No—I mean it, Dakota. It wasn't your fault. Hear me?”

“Whatever.”

“Dammit, girl, you can't save the world. You’re twice as good as most of the best people I know. But you're not God. Okay? And your sister—no, don't hang up. I know you hate talking about it. But listen. Your sister wasn't your damn fault either.”

“Let it go!” she growled.

“Nah, shut up and listen. Neither of them were your fault, Tastee. Sooner you admit it, the sooner you can stop being useless. You have a case to solve—a woman who needs you. Don't let pity kill her. Got me?

I don't care how precious your pain feels—let it go."

And then, to her surprise, he was the one who hung up.

She didn't feel better. But she did feel angry.

Scowling, hands bunched, she surged to her feet, intent on punching something. But Casper was states away. She spat, watching where the first mouthful of beer splattered against the already stained sink. She glared at the sink, her heart pounding, her anger swirling.

She resisted the urge to punch the mirror, still breathing heavily. It took her a couple of seconds to realize this reaction was probably exactly what Casper had been looking for. Anger like this turned her frustration outwards. It was hard to beat up on herself when she so much wanted to punch the mirror or a man or the air.

She did this, twice, swinging her fist through the stale bathroom air with twin shouts. She stopped, breathing heavily.

Casper was an ass. Marcus was an ass for calling him.

But if anyone deserved a beating it was the bastard taking those women, wasn't it? Was she really just wallowing in pity?

She wasn't sure she had much say in her emotions... But Casper was right. She wasn't a quitter. At least—tried not to be. She spat the sour taste from her mouth, turned on the sink, washing the rest of the bottle down the drain. She spun on her heel and marched towards the door. As she passed the trash can she tossed the six pack.

One step at a time. Perhaps they needed to revisit the latest crime scene. Yes... that would be it.

They needed to find the killer. Mostly so she could find someone to punch.

CHAPTER EIGHTEEN

Again, Dakota was grateful when Marcus didn't mention any of it. He just sat in the driver's seat, humming softly as he drove down the highway, heading back in the direction of the latest crime scene once more. As Dakota's gaze traced the land, she ventured to put her near failure in the bathroom behind her. At least for the moment. She was thinking clearly again, which meant Miranda Lopez's life was still in severe danger.

Where was she missing a beat? Why wasn't she seeing clearly? What connected the dots?

Dakota knew people. Studied them. Maybe she had been approaching this all wrong, trying to go through a database, narrowing down a list of unknowns. Perhaps she needed to start with what was known. And start with people. What *she* knew about them.

He was taking drifters, people on the side of the road—defenseless, unaccompanied women. What did that tell her?

Dakota leaned back now, folding her hands in front of her and peering through the windshield as they hastened towards the location where Alison Beswick's body had been found.

Preying on the defenseless, the helpless, under the cover of night could be interpreted as a cautious approach. But then why the motorcycle? Hardly a cautious vehicle. And the witnesses at the crime scenes, according to the reports, had been adamant they'd heard a fleeing motorcycle.

The women were being abducted on the side of the road by this same biker.

So on one hand, his victim choice and time of attack indicated a cautious, hesitant, timid mind. The attacks themselves, and the vehicle used hinted at a brazenness and reckless disregard.

There was a disconnect between how the killer saw himself and how he acted in the world.

Almost certainly a victim of abuse, then. Narcissistic personality disorder or anti-social personality disorder often had formative trauma associated with them. During her schooling, and subsequent training, Dakota had been particularly fascinated by classes on abnormal psychology.

Was the killer acting out some childhood impulse? Was the disconnect between his victim-type and the way he presented himself to the world an indicator of narcissistic tendencies?

Speculation at best. But one thing was certain, the killer was taking drifters and loners. Was he a drifter and loner himself? Perhaps he was seeing companionship in the women he abducted. Temporary companionship. This would fit with the mismatch of perception and reality. Perhaps he felt undeserving of the women he took?

Dakota tapped her fingers against the armrest, shifting uncomfortably as she stared out the window. Growing up, she'd had plenty of experience with would-be Casanovas who spoke a big game, postured and flaunted, but when it came down to an approach or a date request, they quailed. Often in muted, muttered tones, or wandering off into a dark corner of a bar, they'd prey on the less extroverted women, or isolated women who were clearly uncomfortable.

This, in a way, matched the motorcycle killer's MO. All bluster and bravado with his bike, gunning the engine as he sped away from a murder scene, but targeting timidity and loneliness.

Perhaps like those Casanovas, he feared rejection. And, also conducive to trauma, he rejected his captured prize before she could reject him... So he killed and replaced in an endless cycle.

She shuddered at the thought. If this was true, then the chances of him stopping were limited. In fact, he'd only escalate. She knew the type. Behavioral analysts knew the type. They would often take it out easily enough, moving from one bedroom to the next. Hitting on women, seeing them as conquests...

But what if that wasn't an option for this man?

What if he couldn't score a woman's approval to lure her back home? To use her like he would so desperately want?

Impotence? No... Perhaps... but it wouldn't create the same juxtaposition between confidence and sheer timidity in the same way. But what if...

"I... I think he's ugly," she murmured faintly.

She shifted and glanced at Marcus. He raised an eyebrow. "Come again?"

"Our killer, I think he's unattractive. Not just mildly, but blatantly ugly. He might even have some serious disfigurement or exaggerated feature."

Marcus blinked. "What makes you say that?"

“Rejection. He fears rejection.”

“You know this?”

“I think it's likely. There's a mismatch between how he presents himself and the victims he takes.”

“Right... You're thinking atypical attachments? I noticed that too.”

Dakota bobbed her head once, looking off through the glass once more. She didn't want to meet Marcus's searching gaze. Was too embarrassed to.

“Riggs was somewhat good-looking,” Marcus said primly.

Dakota smirked. “You thought Riggs was handsome?” For a brief moment, she felt a flutter of happiness, being able to tease him just like old times.

Marcus rolled his eyes. “He's more your type if I remember correctly.”

Dakota sighed. “The heart wants what it wants...”

Marcus's lips twisted in the faintest smile as well now. He glanced towards her though after a moment, then said, “You know, speaking of Riggs—he mentioned something I thought was interesting.”

“What's that?”

“He said he was a part of a sort of social club for biking enthusiasts.”

Dakota frowned. “Oh?”

“Yeah—called the Crimson Legion. Apparently, they've got a few locations across the Western region.”

“You've been digging?”

He said delicately, “While you were... umm... getting coffee, I looked them up. One of their charters is local. And get this...” He turned to her now. “Two other men on the list we got from the database, before adjusting based on geography, also are members of this Crimson Legion.”

“Two others?”

“That's right. They're not technically a biker gang. They call themselves a club. But they're highly exclusive—a private social club. Members-only at their headquarters.”

Dakota snorted. “So basically a rougher version of an Elks Club?”

“Yeah, something like that.”

Dakota shifted, adjusting her seat belt. “And you're saying three bikers with assault records against women all happen to attend the same place?”

“Yeah... Which got me thinking, you know? Riggs is clear of the abductions, but you floated a theory with the sheriff about multiple sexual assailants. What if a group of these guys are taking turns kidnapping these women, keeping them captive, using them, then disposing of them?"

Dakota shivered in revulsion but tapped her fingers thoughtfully against the glass. "Damn," she muttered. "What if... Crimson Legion you said?"

Marcus gave a quick nod.

"Huh—maybe the crime scene revisit can wait, huh?"

"That's kind of what I was thinking," Agent Clement said. He was already reaching for the GPS on the windshield. As he reprogrammed the device with the new address, Dakota considered the possibilities.

If a private social club, member-exclusive, was targeting women together, then her theory about a single killer didn't fit. Maybe she was just losing her edge.

Three assault records of bikers who all were members of the Crimson Legion, though? Coincidence or pattern?

"I think we should focus on individual assailants," Dakota said at last. "I could be wrong... but... just..." She frowned, shaking her head. "You know what, never mind. Let's go with the group theory."

Marcus shot her a look. A long look, lifting his eyes from the road to survey her. She felt like she wanted to sink into her seat, to hide from his attention.

But after a moment, Marcus gave a faint shake of his head. "No. You're probably right. Let's look at individuals. Maybe jilted or rejected members. Something like that."

Dakota winced. "No—no, I'm sure you're right. I don't know. Let's try your theory and then—"

"Dakota. I trust you," Marcus said simply. "We'll look at individuals."

His tone left no room for debate. She knew what he was trying to do, and as much as she loved him for it, she also felt a heaping dose of terror. What if she was wrong again? Already, evening was rapidly falling. Time was running out for Miranda Lopez.

And again, they were choosing to follow Dakota's lead, her hunch. Was the past clouding her judgment again? Her head felt clearer than it had in months. In no small part thanks to Coach Little's intervention.

But if she was wrong again... if another woman died...

She felt tears threatening her eyes for no reason at all, appearing all of a sudden and causing her to gasp.

She looked sharply away, hiding her face from Marcus as the GPS unit kicked in and the giant FBI agent picked up speed, directing them towards the Crimson Legion's lodge.

CHAPTER NINETEEN

The lodge was hardly impressive. Dakota wrinkled her nose at the cigarette smoke wafting up the stairs from the side stairwell behind the out-building near an old recreational center turned into a private gym. The clubhouse itself was in the basement beneath the gym. The scent of cigarette smoke was mingled with the faint odor of alcohol as the two agents took the stairs slowly.

A couple of men with dark glasses and thick beards and bandannas jostled past, moving up the stairs. One of them still smelled of beer.

They were cackling at some shared joke but when they spotted the two figures in suits, they went suddenly quiet. They glared as they pushed past, up the stairs, moving towards the parking lot.

Dakota suppressed a frown, leaning back against the concrete wall, allowing the men to pass. She ignored their searching glares and suspicious glances. Ahead, she noted a chalkboard boasting half-off menu price for wings. Next to the board was a barred window which reminded her of a jail cell.

At the bottom of the stairs, framed in the entrance, in front of a black-painted door, a tall, muscle-bound man in a green uniform was frowning up at them. "Members only," the big guy said, the words slow as if from lack of use.

"FBI," Marcus called, flashing his credentials. "We need to enter the lodge."

The bouncer didn't budge, crossing his big arms. "Got a warrant?"

Marcus frowned. "We don't need a warrant. Step aside, sir."

The man in the door grunted. "No warrant, no entry. Them's the rules."

Dakota stepped closer to the man now, frowning. A misstep here would be the straw that broke the camel's back no doubt. Already, they were skating on thin ice with Supervising Agent Carter. But three criminals were associated with this place. The sorts of people who beat up on defenseless women. If they'd gone further... namely kidnapping, then waiting for a warrant could prove deadly.

"We won't take long," Dakota said carefully. "We just need to speak with a few of your proprietors."

"Big word. Proprya—what?"

She sighed, jutting a thumb back. "He taught me it."

"Means customers," Marcus called. "Now please step aside. We have probable cause for entry. You're illegally barring federal agents."

The man in the door hesitated, glancing from Dakota to Marcus and back. Dakota didn't want this to come to blows. Any more of that and Marcus's career would be in jeopardy. But they also needed to get past this guard. So she leaned in, muttering, "Know Burt Riggs?"

The man blinked in surprise but covered quickly. "Nope."

"Sure you do. He is a member here. He's now in the hospital. Want to know who put him there?"

The big guy frowned, glancing at the side of Dakota's face. His eyes slipped towards Marcus, but Dakota clicked her tongue. "No—not him. I did. Broke his leg and his bike. We didn't have a warrant then, either. Catch my drift?"

The big guy let out a slow, huffing breath. He glared at her, likely rattled at threats from a woman. Men like this had to be doubly convinced to respect the law if wielded by a female. He gritted his teeth and leaned in as well, whispering fiercely. "Get bent, bitch. No warrant. No entry."

She frowned, feeling a flicker of premonition. Why was he so adamant about guarding the door to a simple lodge?

She studied the profile of his face, inhaling body odor and sweat. Her eyes flicked towards the sealed, darkened door. "What's going on back there?" she asked suddenly.

The bouncer blinked, his mean eyes narrowing. He wrinkled his nose in a sneer to hide the temporary look of concern, but it was too late. Dakota had spotted the fear. Suddenly, the man's hand moved towards his pocket. He began to pull a phone, while simultaneously reaching out to tap against the metal door.

A warning. He wasn't just a guard; he was a signal man.

"No!" Dakota snapped, she tried to grab the phone.

Panicked, he yelled, and his hand darted towards her waist.

He was going for her gun. Dakota's eyes widened. She felt his fingers scramble on the weapon, his own gaze panicked.

She stepped back suddenly—preferring to keep her distance from larger enemies. She moved quickly—he missed her weapon. He snarled, already on a path from which there was no return. He lunged forward. But she was prepared. Her foot snapped up and out, perfect form. Her shin connected and the motion of her blow sent him reeling away from the door, into the gray wall.

He snarled, recovering and trying to swipe at her again.

But this was the reason she'd stepped back.

Now, she retreated again, up two stairs. The man missed, stumbling forward now. She reached out, grabbing his collar and yanking him to the ground. In a swift motion she pivoted around his back, her hand darting towards Marcus, her fingers wiggling insistently.

Agent Clement's handcuffs rattled as he pressed them into her palm, and she hastily cuffed the man on the ground who was groaning and kicking and swallowing dust.

"Hey!" he started shouting. "Hey! Watch out!"

He was pretending to address them, but this, she realized, was also for the sake of the lounge. Quickly, she pushed off the man, leaving him chest-first against the bottom steps, hands secured behind his back. She moved towards the door, shoving it with one shoulder and stepping into a smoke-infused basement.

The Crimson Legion lounge didn't *look* much like a social club.

The low haze, the glass and metal apparatus in the hands of reclining patrons made it look much more like a drug den. A few women with wild hair and far too much makeup were standing against one of the back walls, shifting uncomfortably in outfits that displayed far too much.

The nearest woman had tracks on her arm, her eyes hooded. She couldn't have been much more than a teenager. But a big man with barely any neck was pressing a roll of bills into the hand of another fellow, wearing a suit, behind a podium before reaching out and snaring the arm of the scantily clad young woman.

She protested weakly, blinking as if in a daze, but no one paid much mind.

Other patrons lounged on the leather couches and expensive furniture stationed throughout the room. Some of them were simply smoking blunts, others had small dustings of white powder on glass tables or trays while still others were imbibing or injecting even harder substances.

Most of the occupants in the basement didn't even seem to notice the arrival of the FBI, lost in their own little worlds.

But a few of the basement-dwellers were far more alert. These men were rough, thick with shaved heads, standing throughout the room. All of them were armed, visible by the handguns jutting from their belts or, in one case, gripped in a white-knuckled fist.

One at a time, like slowly turning gargoyles, the armed men with the shaved heads looked in the direction of the two intruders.

The nearest man, with a forehead like a slab of granite, blinked once, twice as if he couldn't quite believe his eyes.

The spring-loaded door behind Dakota and Marcus slowly *thumped* shut.

Agent Clement held up a hand faintly, murmuring, "FBI, everyone stay where you are." At the same time, he reached for his phone, likely to call backup.

The moment his hand entered his pocket, though, Slab-face let loose a whooping bellow. "He's reaching!"

Marcus stepped forward, hands rising in placation. "Hang on—just everyone calm down," he said slowly, eyes shifting about.

The other guards throughout the room were frowning, beginning to move over now. One of the women, who Dakota placed as an unwilling prostitute, was now crying.

Slab-face gave one look at Marcus then pulled his handgun and pointed it at Agent Clement's head. Dakota let out a long sigh, equal parts exasperated and scared.

Marcus went stiff.

Dakota's own weapon was now in her hand, and she aimed past her partner towards the gun-toting guard.

"Drop it!" she snapped.

"You drop it!" he yelled back. "This is private property."

"I can see that," she returned. "Now lower your weapon. Marcus, step to the side." The big man was blocking her line of sight.

But the guard sneered, "Marcus, you move an inch and I lead you up."

"I was just reaching for my phone," Clement said slowly, lifting his device from his pocket now with painstaking motions and wiggling it for all to see. "Just my phone..." She did notice, however, that while he was displaying the device, he was also working the buttons. He'd left the keypad on silent, thankfully.

The other guards, four of them, were quickly approaching, their own weapons now in hand. Dakota felt prickles along her spine, her breath coming in ragged puffs as fear slowly settled like silt.

They'd walked into the lion's den with steaks strapped to their chests. The figures around them were all glaring, their eyes fixated on the intruders. The drug-users, the customers, the prostitutes were nervously edging away from the eye of the storm, slipping out of side doors or, in some cases, so out of it they didn't even seem to notice.

Dakota gripped her weapon tightly. Another shooting would only cause trouble. But more than that, careers weren't the only thing in jeopardy now.

Five men with thick muscles and firearms had now encircled the two agents. Dakota's pulse pounded. Marcus had lowered his phone again. Slab-face was still pointing his weapon at Clement's forehead.

"Get on the ground!" the guard insisted. "Slowly. Kick your weapons towards me!"

"You're under arrest!" Dakota retorted. "Drop your weapon—now!"

"I said get on the ground!"

"Drop your weapon!"

Marcus was still between them both. Voices were rising, followed closely by the tension in the room. A slow, sickly silence descended over the basement. Any moment now, a flick of a finger, a clench of a wrist, a sudden spurt of madness, and it would be the match to ignite the powder keg.

CHAPTER TWENTY

Five guns to two. Not ideal. Dakota slowly lowered her weapon, frowning as she did. "Look—let's talk, alright? No need to get antsy. See, just lower your weapons like me."

They all watched shrewdly as she holstered her gun, breathing heavily at the same time. A calculated risk, but a necessary one. Two to five at such close quarters would just get her and Marcus killed.

"Come on," Dakota said cautiously. "Let's talk. Lower the guns."

Four of the guards slowly directed their weapons towards the ground now, too. They looked more nervous than Slab-face at the notion of accosting two FBI agents. They kept shooting shifty-eyed glances at each other as if searching for backup in their bad decisions.

With four guns facing down, Dakota was able to breath a bit easier. But the air lodged in her throat as she realized Slab-face, the goon who'd first aimed his gun, was still pointing the weapon at Marcus' head.

"Get on the ground!" he repeated. "Now!"

Dakota let out a faint, shuddering breath. It was too much to assume they'd just be allowed to leave and wait for backup. Marcus's phone was still concealed from view, but he'd clearly placed a call. Was backup on its way? How long did they have to stall?

Too long, by the looks of things.

"Look, look," Dakota said quickly, raising her hands and taking a step forward so Marcus was no longer standing between her and Slab-face. "No need to be scared. We just want to talk. Okay? Talk."

She took a faint step forward.

The man who still had his gun raised scowled. "Stop that!" he snapped.

"Of course," she replied in as compliant a tone as she could muster. But she didn't. She stepped forward again.

Fear had to take a backseat in that moment. One thing about contemplating bridges and quick falls—it puts one's survival instinct on a back burner. Now, she was simply concerned for Marcus. Concerned for the women being taken advantage of in the back of the room. Concerned that their killer was somewhere in the audience, watching, waiting. Maybe even Slab-face himself.

The man with the gun shifted his grip, readjusting his aim. Now, instead of pointing the weapon towards Agent Clement, he redirected it towards Dakota.

“Stop right now, bi—”

He didn't finish. Slow, unassuming, presenting as small a threat as possible, followed by a sudden explosion, a volcanic eruption of brutal violence.

It was the advantage she'd always had—being underestimated.

But still, he was bigger, he was armed, he had a gun. She couldn't give him the chance to rise again. So she surged forward all at once. Hand out, flat, knocking the weapon up and off to the side. A sudden *crack.* Bullet missed. Dust fell from the joist above in a trickle.

She was still moving. The gun knocked aside gave her a straight-line towards the man's skull. She brought her elbow swinging forward, the flat connecting with his skull *hard.* One thing about gripping a weapon, it often prevents a rapid response to physical encounter.

Still—she knew it had been risky. Even as the man tottered, blinked, she knew that bullet could've just as easily hit her.

But she'd made her choice. Marcus was safe. She didn't hesitate either to follow with two throat punches. Not intended to *knock* someone out. But to severely incapacitate in as quick a timeframe as possible. The man's eyes were still swimming, now he gurgled, fingers leaping to his throat in desperation. He stumbled back, gagging. His gun hit the floor and she kicked it away.

The man was already falling, toppling to the ground. All of it had only taken a second.

The other guards stared, stunned, uncertain how to react. She waited, breathing heavily. Marcus's voice whispered behind her. “Dakota—careful!”

One of the guards seemed to reach a decision. He began to raise his own gun, his eyes panicking. Dakota cursed, and moved forward again, ducking low, shoulder down. The element of surprise was gone. They were still outnumbered.

Another risk. Calculated, perhaps.

Two of the men reached the opposite conclusion of the new assailant. To them, whatever propelled the thugs to attack wasn't as much of a threat as the idea of being arrested for the murder of feds. So they jammed their weapons into their belts, spun and began sprinting away.

That left two armed men behind. Dakota was bareling into one.

Marcus lunged for the final assailant, tackling him like a football linebacker. The two men hit the ground with a crunching *thud.* For her part, Dakota missed the final man with the gun. He stumbled away from her, yelling and raising his weapon. He fired—a bullet grazed her cheek in white hot pain.

She stared, panicked.

She'd missed. She was too far back.

Marcus was still struggling on the ground with the other thug. But now, Dakota, breathing heavily, her cheek on fire, looked up, staring into the barrel of a weapon pointed between her eyes.

"Die—bitch!" the lodge-member screamed. His finger tightened.

She'd messed up. Miscalculated. Every risk came with multiple paths, possible outcomes. And now she was facing the road less traveled. Training, determination—all of it only prepared a soul. It didn't account for the incalculable.

The finger whitened on the trigger. Dakota braced—only a split second to try and protest.

"Wait—"

She began.

And then something crashed behind her. Voices bellowed into the basement. "Freeze! Police!"

The man pointing the gun at Dakota's head went as still as stone. He gaped at the swarm of officers surging into the basement. Backup. Four, burly cops screamed, "Drop the gun! Drop it or we'll shoot!"

Marcus was busy wrangling the other thug he'd tackled. Dakota just froze, half-couched, breathing heavily, staring into some unseen abyss. Certain she'd been on the verge of reuniting with Carol—after all these years.

It took her a moment to realize just how absent of fear she'd been at the prospect of death. If anything, she almost felt disappointed.

"On the ground! Get on the ground!" The cops were screaming.

Finally, some of the drug-dazed denizens reacted to the incursion of blue. Some of them tried to run. Others just released weary sighs of resignation, sniffing, scooping, or injecting the final contents they could in a half-baked effort to squeeze as much pleasure out of these final moments as possible.

Dakota frowned at where the thug's gun hit the ground. Scowled as he lowered next to it, face against the wooden floor. More shouting. Chaos all around her.

Marcus was rising shakily, dusting himself off and allowing the police to book the man he'd tackled. Other cops were nearing the fallen form of Slab-face. Dakota heard the crackle of radios. Spurting voices. Demands for, "paramedics!"

She felt like a stone in a swirling, storming river.

It all happened so fast...

And she was still alive.

A cruel twist of fate?

Or a mercy?

She shook her head, straightening now, wincing against the pain flaring through her cheek. So close... Yet so far.

"You good?"

She blinked, glancing over towards where Marcus was stomping towards her, his eyes wide with concern as he studied her cheek. "Dakota!"

"Fine!" she said reflexively. "I'm fine—just fine. Only a scrape. I'm fine," she said, numb.

More cops were now appearing at the bottom of the stairs, barreling into the basement. Dakota glanced towards the young prostitute she'd noticed on arrival. The woman was sitting on a couch now, hands in the air, shaking badly, tears streaming down her face.

The big man who'd been trying to drag her away was eating carpet, his arms twisted behind his back.

Dakota felt a strange flush of gratitude.

If she'd had it her way, she would've gone to see Carol. But on the other hand... there were still people here who needed her. People like that woman in the corner of the room.

Dakota jammed her thumbs into her pockets, scowling now as some of the guards were jerked to their feet and shoved towards the basement door.

One of the cops was tugging at her sleeve, saying something that didn't quite register.

She looked around the room, frowning, her thoughts still foggy, adrift. Was their killer down here? Was he hiding in plain sight?

She supposed it was now up to her to answer that very question.

CHAPTER TWENTY ONE

Sirens wailed, bright red and blue lights flickered off the ambulances. Dakota approached the stretcher being dragged towards the nearest opening in the back of an emergency vehicle. Paramedics flanked the stretcher, and the man who she'd throat-punched stared at the sky, blinking as his consciousness slowly returned.

She stalked towards this fellow, eyes narrowed.

Slab-face noticed the motion, glanced over and went suddenly still, intaking air sharply. He muttered something beneath his breath, his voice hoarse, waving a hand urgently as if pleading for the paramedics to hastily place him in the back of the ambulance.

But Dakota moved quicker. She stepped in front of the stretcher, giving a quick shake of her head. "One moment," she said. "BAU," she added.

The paramedics glanced around uncertainly, their eyes finally landing on one of the deputies by the front of the basement entrance. The man gave a quick nod, and the paramedics relaxed, stepping back and allowing Dakota access to the man she'd floored.

"Things aren't looking good for you, hoss," she muttered beneath her breath, staring at the man. She'd hooked her thumbs back in her pants, her shoulders somewhat slumped. Intimidation from a woman on someone like this often put up barriers. She wasn't interested in making a third wave point about her status in society. He was cuffed, headed to a hospital, then jail. That was enough. For now, she needed information.

So she shifted her posture. She began moving furtively, eyes darting back and forth. She projected unease, nervousness.

All a ploy, of course. But intended to allow Slab-face to open up. To put him at ease.

"Imma find you," he rasped, glaring at her from his mean eyes.

Scorn, threats—whatever. As long as he was talking.

She rubbed at her arm nervously. Again, inwardly, she felt nothing. But she needed answers. Needed a lead. The darkening skies were testament to the rapidly dwindling window of time.

"You have an interesting club down there," she muttered. "Probably not going to go well for you. Got a license for that gun?"

"Eat shit, princess."

She tucked a tongue inside her cheek, nodding quickly. "Right, right. I get it. I do. I bet you're used to roughing up ladies. Like those girls you had down there. Or, you know, others..." She trailed off, shaking her head. "I bet you'd like to take a shot at me again, wouldn't you?"

He stared at her from hateful, hooded eyes. He looked mildly confused, as if he couldn't quite figure out what she was up to.

This suited Dakota just fine. "You've been getting new girls recently, huh?" she said noncommittally. "Gifts maybe? Couple of old members bringing 'em by?"

"What? Man—those girls want to be here. They're paid well."

"Sure—sure. They looked ecstatic."

"I don't run this place," he said, wincing and massaging his throat. He glanced towards the nearest paramedic, giving a narrowed eyed glare and a quick flick of his hand like a restaurant-goer calling a waiter.

The paramedic looked away, pretending he hadn't noticed. More lights flashed, sirens peeled as some of the cops tore away from the curb, their back seats stuffed with suspects in cuffs.

Dakota said, "Come on, big guy. You can tell me. Hell, I'll give you my address. Yeah? That way when you're out in fifteen to twenty, you can make good on that promise of finding me." She stared at him, eyes narrowed. "I'll be waiting."

He swallowed again, wetting his damaged throat. He let out a faint grunt, then muttered, "Lady, I'm telling you what it is. Ain't none of those girls come by way of nothin' but pay. All legal."

"Sure, just like the cocaine and meth and illegal gambling, and illegal guns. Super duper legal."

"I don't gotta say nothin' to you. Forget it, lady."

Dakota crossed her arms, shivering somewhat in the descending darkness of the night. She could feel the wind picking up around her. Could feel the cool breeze slipping across her long sleeves. She resisted the urge to roll back the sleeves and show her tattoos to anyone. For now, she blended in just fine.

Camouflage. Hidden in plain sight.

"I get it, I get it," she said, switching tact. "You're no rat."

"Damn sure I ain't."

"Too bad your buddies don't have the same principles."

He frowned, staring at her.

She waved a hand in the direction of a retreating cop car. "Couple of them were jawing before they left. Already about to sign a contract. Leniency in sentencing in order to throw the rest of you guys under the bus. Your noble character will serve you well in prison. I mean, those guys," she waved at the squad car, "will probably get half your sentence. See their girlfriends, the sun—whatever. But you—I respect it. You have your principles."

He glared at her with such venom it sent prickles along her skin. But she didn't back down, didn't change track. Didn't say anything further, preferring to let his little pea-brain reach its own conclusions.

The sirens wailed, tires screeched. A faint hubbub broke out at the bottom of the stairs, leading to the basement, but Dakota couldn't spot the source of the commotion. Likely one of the patrons being booked for drug use.

Not her area. She was after a killer.

The man on the stretcher shifted, wincing as he did. Bruises were already forming on his neck and the tarnished skin shifted with the bobbing of his Adam's apple.

"Shit," he said. "I ain't no rat."

"Course not."

"But..."

"But?"

He wrinkled his nose. "Gotta get me one of those things—what'd you say? Half a sentence."

"Leniency? I'll tell the judge myself."

"Right—I'm no rat."

"So you've said."

"I mean it—I'm not snitching on nobody... just, well, least not nobody that belongs down there. Catch me?"

"I suppose I do," Dakota said, keeping her anticipation in check. "But are you telling me you can think of someone who *doesn't* belong down there who's been trafficking women?"

"Wouldn't call it that," he said quickly.

"What would you call it?"

"Kid named Elvis. Last name some Irish shit. O'Reilly, I think..."

"Elvis O'Reilly. And what are you not ratting on him about?"

The man hesitated, trying to figure out what she'd just said, but it seemed to take too much energy, so in the end he just gave a quick shake of his buzzed head, as if dislodging cobwebs, and said, "We kicked him, lady. Got rid of him quick."

"Yeah? He used to belong to the Crimson Legion?"

The man snorted, then flinched, going still and closing his eyes against a sudden bout of pain. "He didn't belong to nothin'. Bastard kidnapped some doll without our say-so. See me?"

"Yeah, I think I see you." Dakota could now feel her anticipation rising. It came as a prickle across her cheeks, her heart pounding faster.

"So this Elvis guy—who did he kidnap? Was it reported?"

The man on the stretcher snorted. "Shit no... Half sentence, right?"

"Leniency," Dakota said, crossing a finger over her heart and raising it to God.

"Well... Yeah, lady. He kidnapped some girl. Brought her here. Kinda... kinda seemed like he mighta done that thing before. You know. Type of guy who couldn't get a girl on his own."

Dakota blinked. "Was he ugly?"

The man snorted. "I mean... yeah. Dudes are usually ugly, lady. But listen his way ain't how we do things. We pay. We offer. We don't force."

"Sure you don't."

"I'm serious!"

Dakota kept her temper in check and said, through tight lips, "This girl—how come she never reported it?"

"We had a talk...," he muttered with a shrug.

"What sort of talk?"

"Lady, I'm telling you about Elvis. Got me?"

"Let me guess—you threatened to kill her if she told anyone. Is that right?"

"No!" he protested. His eyes screamed yes.

Dakota shook her head, huffing a breath. "This Elvis guy—is he local?"

"Yeah. He's local. He's a douche. Tell him Bradley sent you when you see him, alright?"

Dakota stared, blinking. "Your name is Bradley?"

Before the man could take offense at her tone, the paramedics muttered a quick excuse and an apology. One of the squad cars was blocked by their vehicle and was now leaning on its horn. They once more began to shuffle the stretcher into the back of the vehicle.

"Half sentence!" Bradley shouted.

Dakota flashed a thumbs up, glaring as the man was pushed into the back of the ambulance and the doors were shut one at a time, hiding him in darkness.

Something about it didn't feel right. Helping a man like that.

Offering him medical attention, mercy... Far more than he'd ever offered any of those women downstairs. Dakota sighed, passing a hand over her face and trying to steady herself.

She supposed she owed Bradley some level of gratitude. Elvis O'Reilly, a local, had been kicked from their stupid club for kidnapping a woman. They'd come to the Crimson League looking for their killer.

Had they just found him?

She turned a couple of times, looking for her tall partner. When she spotted him, she waved a hand until he looked over from where he was giving his report to the deputy.

She waved and gestured at him. “Think I got something!” she called.

Marcus gave an apologetic nod to the cop interviewing him, muttered a final comment and then frowned, beginning to move quickly in Dakota's direction. His pace, she guessed, matching her expression—one of urgency.

Darkness was falling.

Time was running out.

CHAPTER TWENTY TWO

Dakota was driving this time, breaking every speed limit she could find. She breezed through a red light, her sirens wailing as she hastened off the boulevard, onto the side street. Tires screeched, rubber met the road as she hastened towards the end of the shabby sub-division.

"Dakota!" Marcus was shouting from the back seat, where his large form sat cramped, one hand raised, gripping the handle above the window, the other holding onto his phone.

"Almost there!" she retorted.

"No—Steele! He's not at his home!"

Dakota frowned, shooting a frantic look into the rearview mirror and staring at her partner. "What?"

"He's not home!" Marcus repeated, his eyes glued to his phone. "They're tracking him. He's—he's not..."

They reached the address for Elvis O'Reilly, kidnapper extraordinaire. A small, single-story house in a run-down subdivision backed against a forest that might have added some level of beauty if not for the heaps of trash and abandoned furniture pieces scattered through the woods. Some people just didn't value the blessing they had.

Dakota scowled as she put the vehicle in park, having pulled right up the driveway to the garage. The house was freshly painted, but tiny. The grass was dry. A picture on the front door read *Beware of Dog*. She could hear the entreaties of said canine braying from the backyard. She heard a jostling chain, more barking.

Now, adrenaline racing, she took a moment to scowl at Marcus Clement. "The tracking came through?"

Marcus bobbed his head hurriedly. "FBI, remember?"

"You sure he's not here?"

She turned, checking the house. The windows were dark. No motion. No movement. More barking from the backyard. No neighbors were out now. At least none she could see.

"That's what it says...," Marcus winced.

Dakota cursed, paused for a moment, then held up a finger. "One sec." She burst through the front door, leaving the engine on and the door swinging. She hastened from the driveway to the small cobblestone path leading to the porch. She reached the door.

Next to the Beware of Dog sign was another with a sketching of a pistol and words that read *We don't call the cops.*

She frowned, but didn't hesitate, hand on her holster, other pounding the door in quick, rapid succession. “Mr. O'Reilly!” she shouted. “FBI!”

Marcus was hastily extricating himself from the back seat. It was slow going, though, sort of like removing sardines from a cramped can. As he disentangled his bulk from the squad car, Dakota pressed the doorbell, pounding the door again.

“O'Reilly!” she shouted.

No response. She frowned, peering through the front windows. Nothing. She glanced at the welcome mat. A pile of uncollected envelopes were stacked together and held by a rubber-band. She glanced off towards the garage, peering through a side window.

The garage was empty.

No car.

Shit. Marcus was right. He wasn't here.

She tried a final time in futility, pounding the door while peering through the large front window. But there was no movement, no response. No car. No one had collected the mail. And Marcus was still calling after her, “He's on the move again, Dakota!”

She cursed, reaching a decision. They'd have to send locals here to search the place just in case, but by the looks of things O'Reilly was squirreled away somewhere else.

Would he be with Miranda?

“Shit—get back in the car!” Dakota called, breaking into a sprint and rushing to the front seat once more. She slipped through the still open door, hitting the vibrating seat from the purring engine, not even taking the time to buckle as she only waited long enough for Marcus's door to slam before squealing out of the drive once more.

“You still got him?” she called, looking in the mirror again, once more flooring the pedal to reach the highway once again.

“Yes! Yes—he's stopped again. It's...,” Marcus frowned. “An abandoned property, looks like. Hard to tell from aerial. A warehouse, maybe?”

Dakota cursed. “Think he's out stalking a new victim?”

“Dunno—I'm calling backup.”

“Send a unit to check out his house. Just in case. Search everything.”

"On it! Dakota—hurry!"

She didn't need a second invitation. Marcus projected the GPS on his phone to the dash system, and she glanced sharply at it, following the bright purple line as it led her away from the house and out of the city once again.

Faster, faster. An abandoned warehouse? Mr. O'Reilly on the move?

She shivered in horror at the thought of what was waiting for them once they reached the location.

***

They sped down a long, dusty road, through an open, chain-link gate with a guard house that looked as if it hadn't been used in years. A fading caution sign had been broken in half, discarded in the middle of the road. The poorly kept asphalt jarred and jounced their vehicle as they bumped along, directed towards the large, square structure against the mountain backdrop.

Evening had fallen completely. Darkness crept into every corner and cranny of the abandoned warehouse ahead of them.

Dakota's eyes glued on the scene, searching desperately for any hint of motion, anything at all. No lights yet. But the tracker was clear. Elvis O'Reilly was somewhere in that dusty building.

"Backup coming?" she muttered as she gritted her teeth and navigated the treacherous, broken-down road leading from the highway through the desert, to the old structure.

"Coming—ten-minute ETA!"

"Shit."

Marcus let out a nervous giggle at the swear as he was oft to do. Dakota glared at the building, fingers tight on the steering wheel. She pulled to a stop in what must have once been an old executive's parking spot. The paint lines were faded, but a small, aluminum sign in front of the curb read "Reserved Parking."

Now, only one other vehicle situated the lot. A motorcycle. A thick, Harley Davidson.

"He's here," she said, jerking her head.

Marcus winced, scowling at the vehicle. "Eight-minute ETA," he replied.

Dakota sat in the seat, door half-open, mind whirring. She scanned the building ahead, the many glass windows, the many entrances and exits. If O'Reilly was waiting for them, or if he'd heard their approach, they'd be walking right into a hail of bullets.

On the other hand, if they didn't move *now* Miranda Lopez could be gasping her last breath.

"We waiting?" Marcus asked, tensed as she was, one arm braced against the door as if preparing to rip it off.

Dakota's sense of urgency, her desperate pace to reach this place had now faded. She felt tense. Her stomach twisting. She stared in the mirror, back at Marcus and winced. "Dammit," she muttered beneath her breath. "What do you think we should do?" she said. Even as she did, it sounded pathetic.

Marcus hesitated, staring at her. She wanted desperately to make a call. To make the right one. But now, sitting there, on the verge of panic and motion, she felt trapped. Should they go in and risk a hail of bullets, along with Marcus's life? Should they wait for backup, risking Miranda? Shit. Shit. SHIT!

No right answer. Just a crossroads. A choice.

And one Marcus was letting her make.

As the silence lingered, the engine cut short, the dust settling around them from their speeding trek over the broken road, Dakota thought she heard something.

She frowned, pushing her door open a bit further, swallowing dusty air, but waving a hand in front of her face to clear her vision.

"What was—"

She began, but then the sound peeled out once more.

A scream. A woman's scream.

"Can't wait!" she said in a fierce whisper. "No time. You got my back?"

"You know it!"

The two of them pushed from their vehicle in tandem, weapons in hands, eyes on the old warehouse, dust whirling about them beneath the evening sky. The cloudy night would have been obscuring enough, but the thin layer of dust, like mist, hovering on the air only further served to obscure their vision. Dakota held back a cough, spitting off to the side, as she and Marcus pressed to the base of the warehouse, stepping along, avoiding windows and moving towards the nearest entrance.

The screaming had faded. But the sound had come from the back of the warehouse, behind what looked like an adjoining workshop or auto center.

The squat, squarish, concrete protrusion had boarded up windows and only a single entrance. A metal door. Would it be locked?

Now, moving silently, foot over foot, Dakota and Marcus hastened towards this closed, steel entrance. No gaps in the boards—no peek through the wood. No sign of Elvis—no sign of his victim. Silence fell heavy and thick, stoppering Dakota's lungs and squeezing rapid gasps from her.

What if she was making a mistake? What if all of this was one huge trap?

Couldn't think like that. Couldn't afford to.

One step at a time. That's all she needed. She wasn't a quitter—that's what Coach had said. He was right, wasn't he?

She felt her shoulders square, her weapon clutched in her grip. They reached the steel door in the squat wing.

The rest of the tall, multi-story warehouse glared down at them, the windows like accusing eyes, fixated on their every move and motion. Dakota's back scraped against rough-concrete as she sidled up to the metal door, one hand braced against her chest, gun gripped tight. Marcus moved quickly, surprisingly light on his feet for such a large fellow.

Once they'd positioned by the door, Dakota met Marcus's gaze. She held it, both their eyes unblinking in the dark. She held up a hand then gestured.

Marcus didn't hesitate. He moved, grabbing the door handle and pulling sharply.

It opened.

CHAPTER TWENTY THREE

Their guns leveled on the room beyond, sweeping through the shadows. Both of them half crouched, motionless, waiting, bodies somewhat turned presenting small targets in the possibility of a barrage of bullets.

It never came.

No movement at first. A faint, glowing yellow light flickered and buzzed, the humming sound coming from the direction of a strange, mechanical machine attached to a conveyor belt. The light flickered above the moving, black belt, illuminating the cramped, dark space.

She swallowed faintly, tasting dust, inhaling the faint odor of mold.

As her eyes adjusted, Dakota suddenly went stiff.

Marcus inhaled sharply.

Both of them were staring at the same source of consternation. A woman tied to a chair in the middle of the room.

Dakota gaped, not quite believing her eyes. The woman almost appeared to be a mannequin, motionless, arms bound to the chair. Her eyes were blindfolded, and she had a gag in her mouth. From here, standing in the door with her gun drawn, Dakota couldn't tell if this was Mrs. Lopez. Was she injured? Too far to tell; she took a step into the cramped space. She heard Marcus's footsteps as he hastily followed. The two of them soldiered into the dark, moving quietly, carefully. Dakota's instincts were on high alert. Part of her wanted to abandon everything, break into a sprint, and rush to the woman's aid. But if this was a trap, if the killer was lurking in the shadows, then it would be doing no one any favors to get all of them killed. As much as it grated, Dakota moved slowly. One step at a time towards the bound woman. There were very few hiding places in the space. Above, she spotted rafters but slits in the metal grate displayed no silhouettes or forms. There were no closets, and no support beams behind which someone might hide. A large double door allowed access to the main building of the warehouse. But these doors were sealed with caution tape over them, undisturbed. Were they alone? Where was Elvis O'Reilly?

She felt Marcus tap her shoulder, and nearly jumped. She glanced back at him, and he was urgently gesturing with his hand for her to move around one side of the room while he began moving towards a low row of workbenches with stray, rusted tools scattering the surface. She frowned, but nodded, sidestepping through the dark, moving in synchronized motion with her partner as they pincered towards the bound woman. Fifteen steps. No sound. Ten. No movement. Five. The woman was now groaning, letting out a faint gasp through her nose.

Dakota couldn't resist. "You're going to be okay," she whispered. "You're going to be fine."

At the voice, the woman suddenly stiffened. She began breathing heavily, her nostrils widening in panic. The light from the conveyor belts illuminated the space. The black rubber guard continued to circle beneath the flickering yellow illumination. Marcus was checking under the workbenches. So far, no reaction. No sign of the killer.

Dakota reached out with trembling fingers and pulled the woman's blindfold down. She felt a jolt of confusion. It wasn't Mrs. Lopez. She pulled at the gag, and the woman gasped desperately. Wide, searching eyes looked Dakota in the face. The woman let out a strangled mewl, and said, "Please, he's coming back any moment. Help me!"

Dakota held a finger to her lips, nodding quickly.

The woman seemed uninjured. Dakota's gaze darted up and down, searching for any sign of bruise or blood.

The woman's eyes were still wide with panic, her hands strained as she tried to tear them from the armrests. The ropes were taught. Dakota reached for her pocket, grasping at the key ring with a utility knife. But as she touched the keys, she heard a sudden *thump*.

Her gaze darted off towards the conveyor belt and then she saw it... almost too late. A dark figure, crouched by an open window, behind the machine. One hand was still braced against the frame, as if he had just slipped into the room. And in his other hand he had a gun.

The shadowed figure steadied, then suddenly began to raise his weapon.

So far, Dakota had managed to avoid getting shot. Her cheek still ached from the graze, but a bullet through the chest was a different matter. She had to act quick. She shouted, "Marcus!" At the same time, she shoved the woman in the chair. No time to untie her. But at least she could push her out of harm's way. Then, Dakota reeled back, her own weapon rising. Too late. The figure in the window squeezed off a shot. A loud blast. Marcus cursed, a rarity for the big man. And he dove beneath the workbench. Dakota was already moving. The bullet hit the floor, sending chips of concrete stinging at her ankles. But she managed to dive on the other side of the large machine with the conveyor belt. She gasped heavily, her cheek pressed against the cold metal. The rough scrape of leather and rubber against her skin as the conveyor belt continued to whir. Marcus was crouched low, gun in hand, desperately aiming in the direction of the window. But the same machine providing cover for Dakota was doing the same for the attacker.

She heard a soft step. Then silence. The figure was waiting. The woman on the ground was sobbing, kicking, struggling. Dakota tried to gesture at her, desperately waving a hand for her to be quiet, to calm. The less attention she drew to herself the better.

But the woman was too panicked. Dakota couldn't let her kick and buck, exposed, right in the line of fire. If she didn't do something, the killer might just take her out while they watched. But Dakota was pinned.

She needed to distract him. To redirect his attention from his would-be victim. "Elvis?" she called.

She heard the faintest intake of breath.

"Yeah," she called, "We know it's you. Cops are surrounding this place. You have no way out. Put down your gun."

No response.

She gritted her teeth in frustration. Her own weapon was clutched tight. She waited, tentative, as patient as possible. No response.

Then, another gunshot. This time, a bullet punctured through the machine above her, and a large dent slammed into one side of the metal container. She cursed, ducking even lower, using the metal flank of the machine for as much coverage she could manage. Marcus held a finger to his lips but was now circling to the other side of the machine where there was a gap in the wall. He would face the window, then. But it was slow going, keeping low, quiet, not drawing attention. Dakota decided to camouflage his footsteps with another shout. "The lounge sold you out. Is that why you've been killing women? Pity party because they kicked you out?"

She seemed to have hit a nerve. The man on the other side of the machine growled. "I left," he said in a sort of lazy drawl. "No one kicked me out."

He had a young voice. A sneering voice. The sort of voice that might have belonged in a country club among an Ivy League audience. But now, here, in a dusty, abandoned warehouse, it seemed a frail, thin tone.

"Come on," Dakota wheedled, still trying to distract him as Marcus moved in a crouch. "You can tell me the truth. You have to kidnap and kill them because women won't go with you voluntarily, is that right?"

"How about you shut up and show yourself. If you don't, I'm going to shoot the lady."

The woman struggling on the toppled chair went stiff, her eyes wide in the dark. Dakota resisted the urge to curse beneath her breath. "The building is surrounded, Elvis."

"Liar," the man said with a wicked chuckle. "I saw that big guy come in. He there too?"

Marcus didn't say a word, he had nearly reached the gap at the other side of the machine. Dakota wondered if he would have a clear shot towards the window. By the sound of things, the killer hadn't moved.

"Elvis," she said, conversationally, "you don't want to do anything stupid. You can still get out of this alive."

"Same to you," he retorted. "Just put your gun down. You cops? Sheriff department?"

"FBI," she retorted.

He made no effort to conceal the blurted curse word.

"That's right," she said. "We've been tracking you. There's nowhere to go, Elvis. You don't need to kill her. There's been enough murders, haven't there?"

"Stop it," he snapped. "I don't know what you gonna peg me for. But I haven't killed anyone recently."

"Recently?"

"At all," he amended. Then, sarcastically, he added, "Oops."

Dakota was beginning to loathe this fellow more and more. "I mean it," she said. "Throw your gun away. This doesn't have to end badly."

He retorted, "I'll give you a count of five before I put a bullet in her head. Got me? Come out with your hands up."

"Hang on," Dakota said desperately. Marcus had reached the edge of the machine. Gun in hand. He began slowly to edge around, aiming.

"Five."

"Calm down."

"Four."

Marcus's arm extended. He frowned, quizzically, as if he couldn't quite see the killer just yet.

"Three."

"I don't know what you're calling recent," Dakota said, shouting the first thing that came to mind. "You don't think Allison was recent? What about Michayla?"

A pause. "I read about them. The motorcycle killer. Also, *two*."

Dakota winced, hissing sharply. "Yeah. Your other victims."

The young man with the gun let loose a faint giggle. "Hang on, what? I didn't kill them. This little gift on the ground was just to get me back in the good graces with the league. They like fresh meat. One."

A gunshot.

Dakota's heart leapt. She heard a sudden thump. The sound of a clatter. She exhaled rapidly, staring towards the woman lying on the ground who had gone suddenly still. Tense. Panicked. Eyes still open, but very much alive.

Marcus, on the other hand, looked at death's door. Frozen, horrified. His hand extended, gun clutched. He seemed to have forgotten to breathe.

Dakota stared. "Get him?"

Marcus was moving again, shoving through the small gap, pushing towards the window. Dakota cursed, rounding the other side of the machine. And then she saw him. A man with blonde, short-cut hair, lying face down in a pool of blood. His gun lay off to the side. The window was open behind him, the blinds fluttering softly.

Marcus was barking instructions into his phone. The big man still looked panicked. She knew he didn't like pulling the trigger. Marcus had joined the force to help the living. To protect. Dakota had joined to catch the bad guys.

“He hit his head!” Marcus shouted desperately. “Hello!” he slapped the man's face. “I—he's breathing! Thank God.”

“Sure as hell looks like you shot him!” Dakota retorted, busy herself.

“Shoulder—just the shoulder. He fell and hit his head...,” Marcus suddenly sighed in relief. “Thank God he's breathing. He's unconscious.” The big man was now applying pressure to the shoulder wound, stopping the blood. At the same time, his other hand probed Elvis's head where he'd struck the machine and fell.

Now, as Marcus tried to apply first-aid to the man he'd shot, Dakota didn't even look at his face. She didn't care. She was busy reaching for her utility knife, sawing at the ropes that secured the kidnapped woman's arms. She kept murmuring, her words coming quick, "It's going to be okay. You're fine. You're okay. You're safe now. I promise."

Once she had cut through the ropes, the woman let out a squealing sob, and tucked her legs up under her, hugging them against her body. She lay on the cold ground, sobbing horribly. Dakota awkwardly crouched next to her, one hand extended, tentatively pressed against the woman's arm in a comforting gesture.

Marcus's voice was shaking badly as he called for paramedics. Dakota just crouched, back to the killer, facing his would-be victim. Inwardly, she felt a sudden surge of relief. She'd saved someone. Well, Marcus had. But she'd been a part of it. This time, it hadn't ended in death. But where was Mrs. Lopez? Was this a new victim? Had Mr. O'Reilly already killed Miranda?

"Are you okay?" Dakota said, checking again. The woman was still shaking. Tears streamed down her cheeks. "Did he hurt you?"

She gave a sniff and a quick shake of her head. "He was going to," she stammered. "But you got here in time."

"I'm very sorry. Please. I need you to be strong. There's another woman out there. Did you see her? Did he say anything about her?"

"He, he didn't say anything. He drugged me at a bar. I thought we were going back to his place. But he brought me here."

Dakota frowned now. That did not fit the MO.

"Miranda Lopez? Did you hear about her?"

The woman just shook her head, trembling horribly. She sobbed again.

Dakota frowned, and only now did she glance back at the killer. In a pool of his own blood, face down. Marcus had managed to stop the shoulder from bleeding and was now tending to the head wound. At least this time she hadn't pulled the trigger. A strange thing to think. But, for Marcus's career, it was oddly better that he'd shot the man, not Dakota.

A callous, heartless thought. She felt a pang of guilt. What was this job doing to her?

She could feel the woman trembling beneath her hand. And at the same time, she felt a jarring uncertainty. No sign of Miss Lopez. Drugged in a bar. Not picked up on the side of the road. And the killer's words were clear. He didn't know anything about the murders. At least not recently. Why would he lie? He was willing to kill her, to die in a gunfight. What reason did he have to lie?

It didn't fit the MO.

“Marcus—any chance he wakes?”

“He's out. I don't know—but he'll be fine.” Marcus sounded more relieved than Dakota would ever have been crouched over a scumbag.

Dakota returned her attention to the person at hand. "I'm sorry, ma'am, how old are you?"

The trembling woman on the ground looked up, through teary eyes. She allowed herself to be helped into a sitting position. Inhaling shakily, she gasped, "Forty-one."

Dakota frowned. Too old. The killer was taking twenty-year-olds. He was taking hitchhikers. He wasn't drugging them in bars. He wasn't taking women in their forties.

A slow, thick weight of dread filled her stomach.

"Marcus, we need to speak with him. Is he gonna make it?"

Agent Clement was busy, using everything he seemed to remember from a training manual to bandage the injured shooter. The man's gun was kicked off to the side, beneath the window. In the distance, Dakota thought she heard sirens.

"Marcus?" she insisted.

"He'll be fine," he retorted. "Give me a moment."

"We don't have a moment. I don't think this is our guy."

Marcus looked over, eyes bugging in horror. "What?

"It doesn't fit. Marcus, I don't think this is him."

"Shut up," he retorted. Just as quickly, he winced, shaking his head apologetically. "Sorry, sorry," he murmured, even while still ministering to their attacker. "It has to be him."

"It doesn't fit."

"I shot him, Dakota. It's him."

Dakota pressed her lips. She didn't say anything. Marcus would get over it eventually. He had to. He'd shot a man shooting at her. Killer or not, it was either the victim or the victimizer. He hadn't had a choice. Eventually he would see it that way. But Marcus had always been sensitive. It would take time. The sirens in the distance were getting closer. She wouldn't be able to interrogate him until he regained consciousness. If he did... that was a lot of blood. Which meant she had to make a call. Another crossroads. Another branching path. Had he been lying? Was this just a deviation? He had deviated before by picking Mrs. Lopez as a victim, instead of just a drifter or hitchhiker. On the other hand, the woman didn't fit. She was too old. The MO didn't fit. He had denied having anything to do with the other murders. He didn't have a reason to lie if he was willing to die by cop.

A crossroads. A decision.

Was she wrong?

Dammit.

She had to think. She had to think quickly.

Time was of the essence. Was Miranda dead? Or was she still out there, desperately hoping, waiting for someone to rescue her?

Was the motorcycle killer bleeding now, on the concrete floor? Or was he alive and well, preparing for another hunt?

A crossroads. A choice. And again, it was all down to her.

CHAPTER TWENTY FOUR

Her arms ached, and sweat trickled down the side of her face, beading at the edge of her chin. She could feel her ribs straining against her skin. Could feel her heart pounding wildly, her adrenaline rushing through her body; she wanted nothing more than to be cut free. But the pleading desperation didn't matter. He'd hurt her. Pain extended down her arms. She could feel blood on her legs. Before he'd really gotten into it, though, he'd received a notification on his phone. She could hear him now in the other room watching the TV. It sounded like he was keeping track of the news.

She had strained to listen as well, desperately hopeful that someone was coming for her, but it was no use. She had only picked up faint clips of the news station through the vent. Something about a brawl at a basement bar. Not long ago, something else about a shooting in a warehouse. But none of it would help Miranda. She thought of Miguel, her son—she pictured the small child wiggling in her husband's lap. Pictured his smile, twinkling eyes and dimpled cheeks. It was the only thing that prevented her from descending into madness. Her shoulders felt like they might already be out of socket. She just wanted to go to sleep. It was just so much pain.

And then she heard the click of the lock. Her heart jolted. She glanced sharply at the door which creaked as it opened. The man with the long hair and the scarred face suddenly emerged in the room once more. He moved through the motorcycle parts discarded through the room like a practiced tracker navigating underbrush.

His eyes were on her, now. His teeth set.

"Please," she said desperately. "Please, just let me go."

He ignored her. Didn't speak. His eyes narrowed. "Say the words," he said at last. "Ask me. Say it."

She trembled. She knew what he wanted. He'd spelled it out clearly enough. He wanted her to beg him to kill her. He had threatened to do all sorts of nasty things. Things that made her blood curdle. Unless she asked to be killed, he had promised to hurt her.

He had even started to, and then the notification had come in. But now he was back. There was nowhere for her to run. No more beeping news bulletins. Nothing to do but cry and plead.

But her entreaties didn't matter to him.

"Say it," he insisted. "Ask me to kill you. It will be quick. You never let it be quick with me. You started this. This is your fault."

He sometimes spoke like this, but she couldn't figure out what he meant. The man was clearly deranged. He limped closer to her, scowling. His breath smelled faintly of mint. "Say it," he whispered. "It will all be over so soon."

She frowned, trying to rearrange her features into something like a decipherable expression. "I don't know you," she insisted. "I'm sorry if you were hurt. But I don't know you."

His eyes suddenly widened in rage. He struck her, hard. He screamed in her face, saliva flying. "You're sorry? You dare say you're sorry?"

He threw back his head and laughed. He struck her again. Her face was so numb, though, the pain almost didn't register.

He spun on his heel, shaking his head rapidly, and muttering beneath his breath. "Sorry. You've never been sorry. I'll make you sorry. You're not even the right one. I'm going to replace you. I'm going to find a better one. And then she will squeal. Sorry. What a stupid thing to say."

He was rambling now, ranting, raging.

She whimpered, trying to plead, to get a word in edgewise. Speaking meant pain. Upsetting him meant pain. But she needed to get back to her husband. Needed to get back to her son. This couldn't be how it ended. Not this way. Not yet. She offered up a small prayer, wishing she could cross herself. Her fingers flicked reflexively above the ropes.

The killer was still muttering darkly but was now reaching for the helmet on the workbench.

"Please," she said. "Just let me go."

"You better believe I'll let you go," he sneered. "I'll show you what I think of your apology. After all these years. You dare," he growled. He spat, place the helmet on his head, secure his gloves, and began marching away.

"I'll find another. And then I'll get rid of you. And I won't stop until you beg me to kill you. Understand? And I'm so very *sorry*," he added sarcastically. "But I can't stand the sight of you. I'm going to kill you the quickest out of all of them."

He let out a long sigh of satisfaction, an almost orgasmic sound.

"But first I have to find another. That's how it is."

She couldn't see his expression now. It almost sounded like he was smiling. She tried to plead, whimpering, but it was no use. He turned on his heel and began marching away. Muttering darkly beneath his breath a series of expletives.

She groaned, tears streaking her cheek. The sweat mingled on her chin with the teardrops.

He'd made this clear as well. If he found someone else, he was going to kill her. That's what he'd said he done to another woman. That poor soul.

Miranda let out a shuddering gasp and murmured another prayer. Desperate, hopeful that she had been given another few minutes without pain. But when he returned, if he found someone else.

There would be no stopping him.

CHAPTER TWENTY FIVE

Dakota lingered by their borrowed sedan in the parking lot, facing the executive spot.

Cop cars and ambulances and FBI vehicles were surrounding the warehouse. Light patterns flashed across the evening clouds. Marcus was standing near one of the ambulances, speaking in grave tones to three officers and two agents. They were grilling him about the shooting. Elvis O'Reilly was on his way to the hospital. Still unconscious. No dice for an interrogation.

Which was why Dakota was standing in the shadows, lingering. The victim had long since been rushed to a hospital also; she was going to be fine according to the paramedics. A silver lining. A much needed one. But one that had given Dakota a glimpse of hope. A strange glimpse. One she wasn't much accustomed to.

And now she had a choice to make. The FBI, the sheriff, the deputies, the local boys and girls in blue, and even Marcus, all seemed to have reached the conclusion that they'd found the motorcycle killer. There was even some talk about releasing this to the news.

But Dakota wasn't so sure. Wrong age. Wrong MO. He had denied it.

Scant evidence, perhaps. But not insubstantial.

He was still out there. He was still stalking. Besides, what would the harm be to double check? If she was wrong, then she would just waste her own time. Who cared? It wasn't like she would do anything productive back in a hotel. But if she was right, that meant there was still hope. Hope that Mrs. Lopez hadn't been killed already. No sightings of a body at a rest stop. No one reporting the sound of a motorcycle fleeing a crime scene. He hadn't hidden the bodies before. So if Miranda was dead, where was she?

Dakota reached a decision.

Marcus would have to get a ride back on his own. If she told him what she was going to do, there was no way he'd allow it. But she had come too far. She had to make sure. She had to try and find Miranda.

There was something intoxicating about saving a life. And she considered that word intentionally in her thoughts. Intoxicating.

Somehow, seeing that look of hope in the woman's face as Dakota had cut her bindings free, it had pushed back the darkness

She didn't want to admit it as she put the vehicle in gear, and began to pull out of the parking spot, but in a way, she was chasing a rush. The rush of saving a life and catching a bad guy.

If it worked, it worked.

And Dakota could think of only one way to find the killer now. Not a list. Not a database. Not by out-thinking. But the old-fashioned way. Direct confrontation. Person to person. Men often underestimated her. They saw a woman, with average height, a scar, a lumpy ear from her boxing days, and not much else. They didn't see a threat.

So maybe it was time for her to use that to her own advantage.

The killer hunted long, desolate roads through the heart of Nevada. By scouring the database for potential killers, she had grown familiar with the paths the killer had taken. She couldn't predict exactly, but he would be looking again. News of the motorcycle killer was all across the state. Pickings would be slim.

But what if she gave him the exact bait he was looking for? She wasn't twenty, but fairly attractive. Sometimes, looks could be construed for youth, especially at night.

She would have to leave her gun in the car. Her badge too. Marcus would kill her if he knew what she was thinking.

"I'm not a quitter," she murmured to herself.

Coach Little had told her that. He'd been right. She wasn't sure he would be thrilled at the prospect of using herself as bait. But this was a rush worth chasing. And this time no one could stop her. It was to save a life, after all. How could that be bad?

She began picking up the pace, tearing out of the parking lot, swerving to avoid a parked SUV on the side of the road. She sped up the dusty path back towards the chain-link fence. Faster, faster, past the abandoned guardhouse. Faster.

Her heart in her throat.

She knew where she was going. The same road where he had taken Michayla. That was the longest road. The most desolate. The best hunting grounds for a hunter being chased. The killer was smart. He'd proven that. He was subtle. He would avoid most of the populated areas. And two of the roads he'd been hunting now had police blockades on them following the discovery of Alison's body. There was only one option. A long, desolate stretch of Nevada Highway through the desert.

He would come. He would hunt.

And this time, someone would be waiting for him.

Faster, faster, she picked up speed, hastening out into the night, and towards her destination. Not nearly a destination. More of a direction. Miles and miles of open asphalt.

She knew what she had to do.

***

The wind howled. The night hung dark and thick. The clouds obscured the stars and the moon. No safety lights. Not as far as the eye could see. Perfect. It would help her stand out.

Dakota shivered at the wind whistling through her cracked window. The frigid breeze pawed at her wounded cheek. She winced against the pain, hoping desperately it wouldn't turn the killer off to her.

No matter. She'd already made up her mind.

She reached into the dashboard, pulling out the small flashlight. She placed her gun, her wallet, and her identification into the compartment and closed it. Then she pushed out of the car. The door shut. Caught by the wind. She locked it. And then turned to face the road.

No cars had passed in a while. In the distance, she spotted the outline of a fleeing truck. But otherwise, there was only desolation.

Loneliness. Something about the stretch of road reminded her of her nighttime dreams.

She lifted her phone, her fingers cold. She texted Marcus her location, pinging it. She added a text. *Sorry. I had to.*

She sent it, then put her phone on silent, jammed it into her pocket, and turned on her flashlight.

She couldn't use the gun. Couldn't have the FBI identification. She needed him to take her to Miranda. If he thought for a second that she was law enforcement he might just kill her there, or flee. No. She needed him to think he had the upper hand. It was the only way.

She started to march, flashlight flickering in her hand, swishing across the long, dusty gray road. She picked up the pace, moving as quickly as she could, along the side of the road, making sure her light caught the clouds.

Now, all that remained was a little bit of patience. He would be out tonight. She knew it. They hadn't caught the killer. He would hunt. And she would make every effort to entice him.

Gravel crunched, the wind whipped, and the darkness encroached around her.

She glimpsed headlights behind her. Two of them, though. The rumble of an engine, the whir of a machine. A sedan sped past her, going ten over, heading in the direction of the truck. Just as quickly as it had come, it vanished. Here one moment, gone the next. Strange. So strange how quickly things can vanish.

A lot of things got lost out in the Nevada desert.

She continued walking, still waving her light, like a signal, a beacon. One thing was good about these desolate lanes; the killer would have a hard time finding a target as well. The two closed roads would make it impossible for him. Motorcycles were being stopped. Riders checked. This Highway was his only option. Would he smell the trap? Would he know that Dakota had actively set up the roadblocks?

No. The police were already hinting to the news that they had caught the killer. That would only put the real murderer at ease. It might enrage him, which would be good too. He would make a mistake.

Another flash of headlights behind her. This time a single headlight. Her heart jumped, she turned sharply.

No; just a truck. One of the headlights broken. The vehicle began to slow as it approached her. Her heart pounded. But then it picked up the pace again, edging to the opposite side of the road, to avoid collision. And then it leaned on its horn as if in frustration and sped away again. After a few seconds, she was alone once more.

There was something cathartic about walking in the dark. Something almost peaceful, tranquil about moving away from anything and everyone. Marching into danger.

She wasn't sure how long she'd been walking. Time seemed to slow. She could feel the urgency of the moment pressing in on her, crushing her. What would she do if Miranda was already dead? What could she do? It was almost like watching a car crash in slow motion. Except the vehicle was her life, and the impact was her decision making. She knew what she was going to do. She knew how she would medicate. She knew the inevitable despair. She knew the sadness. And yet it would all happen anyway. Knowing about it would never prevent it. Never had.

She sighed, inhaling the cold mountain air.

And then she heard a growl

A mountain lion? No. A grumble of an engine. Coming from the other direction, on the other side of the road. Whoever was approaching would've had a full view of her flashing light.

Dakota tensed. A single headlight, emerging over the hill. No cars behind her. No cars ahead. The grumbling, growling engine grew nearer.

Her skin prickled. Her heart pounded. For one wild moment, she thought to turn and flee. But she had chosen this gambit. She had chosen to risk. She needed him to take her to Mrs. Lopez. She couldn't spook him. Couldn't let him use promises of delivering a location as leverage. Killers had done that in the past, only leading investigators on until their victims died of dehydration.

Miranda had to be alive. Dakota couldn't allow herself to think otherwise.

The grumbling engine slowed. The bright headlight dimmed. A motorcycle rider came alongside her, on the opposite side of the road. The man wore a dark helmet, dark, leather gloves, and a wind breaker. He sat on the bike, his foot skipping a couple of times as he came to a full stop, balancing the weight of the machine. And then he just stood there, waiting quietly.

She aimed the lights towards his feet, and hung her head somewhat, so he wouldn't see too clearly.

"Hello," she called out tentatively.

He didn't say anything. Didn't gesture. Didn't move.

"My car broke down," she tried again. She flashed her light back down the long shoulder of the road. She was surprised to see just how far away the vehicle was. Good thing, too. The undercover cop car wouldn't be obvious at first glance. But under close scrutiny, someone could figure out what it was.

"Do you think you could give me a ride?" she said hesitantly. Was this the man? Why wasn't he saying anything? Could he really be the killer? Right now he just seemed like a weirdo. Wouldn't a killer be more forward than this?

She glanced back. Nothing behind her. Glanced ahead. Nothing.

This was her only option. And yet still he just sat there, waiting, as if hoping for some cue.

She took a tentative step towards him, raising her flashlight to illuminate him.

"My name is Dakota," she said. "What's yours?"

She played the docile sheep well enough. A faint quaver to her tone. Her shoulders somewhat hunched. Her expression shy. She didn't just study people. Didn't just watch their movements, their muscles, their twitches, their motions. She could also display it. Useful. Tactical. And right now, she wasn't sure whether or not it was working.

Suddenly, a faint voice called, "How old are you?"

The tone was muffled by the helmet. The voice carried an odd rasp.

"Not very appropriate," she said, sheepishly. "You know what, maybe I'm fine."

She faked a turn as if she were about to start walking away again.

"Sorry," he called back urgently.

She paused, allowing the man to buy the act. There it was. In his tone. He was pretending like he didn't want anything from her. But his sudden reaction suggested otherwise. His flesh was screaming. He was desperate. This was the bastard.

She turned back, shrugging her shoulder once. "I'm twenty-eight," she said. A lie. But the killer had a type.

He went silent again. He was playing a role. Stoic, scary. Did this really work? She supposed it might, on someone desperate enough to need help. Ought she just arrest him then and there? no... No not if Miranda was in a bad way. There might not be enough time for an arrest, a drive to the station, a long, arduous interrogation with red tape and lawyers. No—saving lives was intoxicating, so Dakota would have to do what was necessary.

Part of her wanted to just roll her eyes. The motorcycle rider wasn't nearly as mysterious as he thought he was. That stupid helmet didn't hide too much of the ego on display. It was almost like he wanted her to ask him for a ride. Please sir, torture me and kill me. Was that what he wanted?

She sighed. If it got her to Miranda, maybe it was the best option.

"Think you could give me a lift?" she said, taking another step forward.

His gloved hand patted the seat behind him.

This was it. This was him. Her heart skipped. She swallowed. She would have to be on her game from this moment forward. She would have to be on the lookout for everything. She was leaving her gun behind. She still had her keys. But chances were, he would confiscate those before he brought her to his lair. She needed to see where that was. And so, trembling, she approached the bike and its silent rider. She slipped onto the back and was surprised that he didn't react. Didn't attack, didn't pull at her. He just let her straddle the seat.

Tentatively she reached out, placing her hands on the man's shoulders. The only grip there was. The moment she did, he took off like a rocket. As if this was the intention all along.

Her stomach twisted, her grip tightened on his shoulders. Faster, faster. They were picking up speed now. Faintly, she almost felt him vibrate as if he were chuckling. No, just the engine. Or maybe...

Suddenly, one of his hands reached up and yanked hard at her arm. He jerked her hand around his waist, and then held it there, in a vice-like grip.

This was it. She'd found him. Now, she would just have to hope he was taking her where she needed to go.

The speed didn't bother her. The tight grip on her wrist didn't matter. The pain along her cheek was irrelevant. Faster, faster, through the dark of night, through the Nevada desert, off to some unknown location.

She was alone. No backup.

But there was still a chance she could save Mrs. Lopez. Still a chance that she could make up for...

For what?

Suddenly it struck her just how stupid this plan was. How much danger she really was in.

But there was no time for regrets.

The howl of the wind, the rush of rubber against asphalt, the tense grip of her fingers, none of it allowed for second thoughts. She'd made her choice. Now she just had to survive.

CHAPTER TWENTY SIX

Dakota tensed, staring across the long, dusty road illuminated by the headlight of the motorcycle. She could feel their speed slowing. For nearly five minutes now, he'd taken them off road. Ahead, she spotted what looked like an old auto shop. A small house sat next to the building. She glimpsed broken down portions of metal and wooden fence in the distance, demarcating acreage. There were no lights save the single orange glow emanating from one of the auto shop's windows. The building itself looked like it hadn't been used in years.

But as they drew closer, and as the man on the bike slowed his vehicle, her rising sense of apprehension and horror reached a crescendo. Her stomach twisted. The man bumped the kickstand and brought the bike to a halt in front of a sliding metal door. He didn't speak. He still gripped her wrist, hard. But as he dismounted, his motions were cocky. He was confident he was stronger than her. Confident he could control her. Certain there was nothing she could do to stop him. And for the moment, she needed to play along. She still hadn't found Mrs. Lopez.

"Please," she said, keeping up the act. "Where are we?"

"Shut up, whore," he snapped. Now that they were off the main road, isolated, he seemed to find some confidence. This, she thought in the back of her mind, fit her theory about his mismatched behavioral patterns.

She allowed the man to drag her off the bike as well; suddenly, his hand darted forward, and he began rummaging in her pockets.

She tensed, instinctively holding back the urge to punch him in the nose.

He took her phone, turned it off, and then put it in his own pocket. He found the keys with the knife and pocketed those as well. Once he was done, he reached into the metal post slot in the sliding door and pulled out a long cord of rope.

"Stay still," he growled.

Dakota protested, playing the part. At the same time, her eyes darted around, searching desperately for any sign of the missing woman. Her fear for her own safety was on the back burner. She had been taken miles from the road where she'd abandoned her car. Now her phone was off; she was alone.

"Stop struggling," he growled. He spoke those words in a very practiced way. Chills crept across her arms. And it took everything in her not to lash out at the source of fear. The man in the motorcycle helmet ripped her arms behind her back, and she could feel the rope biting into her wrists.

"Please, what are you doing?" she protested.

He was chuckling now. He was enjoying her fear. They often did.

The rope suddenly went taut. His hand gripped her shoulder and shoved her, hard. She stumbled forward.

And then he began to speak, his voice laden with humor and contempt. "You and I are going to have some fun," he said. "Remember all those times you brought the men home? I told you they were hurting me. I told you they weren't safe. Well, now I am not *safe*."

Dakota wrinkled her nose. The man was clearly suffering some type of break. She'd been right about that as well.

Not that it would matter much if she didn't get out alive.

Still, she tried to focus, looking around.

"Are we alone?" she said in a pleading voice. Really, she was looking for information.

He just shook his head, spitting off to the side. "You never could handle loneliness. That's what makes you a slut; you let men come through like you were some national park. You didn't care what they did to me. You didn't care that they hurt me. Did you, bitch!"

He shoved her again and this time she slammed into the sliding metal door. He reached it, gripped the handle, and with a growl, yanked it up. Only then, as he moved inward, did she notice his limp.

He pushed her past a couch beneath a glowing TV, towards a second metal door. This one bolted on the inside.

He unlocked the bolt, yanked the door open, and said, "Want to meet the woman you're replacing?" He giggled now. "You had so many of them come through. You couldn't just choose one. So many. I'm just doing the same thing you did."

Dakota outwardly presented fear. This wasn't difficult to do. But at the same time, she tried to pay attention to her surroundings. The television was showing a news station. As he pushed her through the door, though, she emerged in what looked like a garage, scattered with motorcycle parts. There were workbenches, tools, buckets of washers and screws and the like.

There was also a woman dangling from the ceiling, her arms held above her head by rope.

Dakota tensed. It was Mrs. Lopez.

Dakota's own hands were painfully tied behind her back.

The killer didn't seem to realize the shift in his newest victim's posture. He kept dragging her forward, but Dakota was now bracing herself. Preparing. She glanced around the room for a possible sharp edge to unbind her hands.

"Guess what I found?" he called towards the dangling woman. "Now you and I are going to have some fun for a few hours. I won't replace you until you tell me to. That's my word. I won't break it. This is going to be very enjoyable. Normally they break quick. You, new whore, you get to watch me do some things. You're gonna like it."

He giggled, and suddenly shoved Dakota, hard. She stumbled against one of the workbenches, nearly falling. She couldn't quite catch her balance with her bound hands and winced where her hip collided with the jutting wood. At the same time, the killer ripped his helmet off, revealing a horribly disfigured, scarred face. Long, silky smooth, brown hair attempted to obscure the injury, but failed. His face was creased in a rage, and he snatched a knife off the nearest table. Chuckling to himself, he began stomping towards Miranda. She squealed in fright. Desperately, she shouted, pleading. "Please," she moaned. "Please don't hurt me. I have a family!"

"What are the magic words?" the killer asked in a singsong voice. He limped as he moved. "Three little words. And this can all be over."

Miranda whimpered but sealed her lips.

Dakota tried to push up, her bound hands making it difficult. She growled, looking around for a saw blade, something. There, a jigsaw. But no, too far on the table, she couldn't reach it.

Now, he had reached Miranda, weapon extended towards her stomach. He was making shushing sounds, grinning widely as he did. The jack-o'-lantern leer of his scarred face twisted the burnt flesh. Miranda tried to withdraw, trying to kick. But he caught her leg, holding it tight.

"I have all the time in the world," he sneered up at her. "You saw that. When he made me like this."

The knife descended, fast.

Dakota yelled.

Miranda screamed.

***

Agent Marcus Clement broke into a sprint and threw himself into a vehicle the second he saw the text message. He didn't care about the cops behind him. Didn't care about the stuttered protest from the FBI agent taking his report. The FBI agent had left her keys in the car. Marcus would have to apologize later. It all could wait. *She* was doing something stupid. He should've known to keep an eye on her. He was the one who'd brought her back into this. If anything happened to her, it was his fault. He would have to answer to Coach Little, but even worse, he would have to answer to his own conscience.

The engine roared as he rushed towards the locator on Dakota's car. She wasn't that far... At least she'd decided to do something locally stupid.

He hated what had happened back there. Hated that he had just shot a man. He wished he could've figured out another way to bring it to a peaceful end.

But sometimes, even Marcus had to admit idealistic thinking could only get so far.

"Come on," he muttered beneath his breath. "Come on," he said louder.

He sped through the night, hastening rapidly towards the location Dakota had pinged. Would she still be there? He couldn't believe she was doing *this*. Granted, she had always been willing to take risks in the past.

No. He couldn't just get there and try to read the dusty ground like some sort of Texas Ranger. He needed help. So he ripped his phone from his pocket, still speeding, and dialed. They could track phones now. Even if they were turned off. They'd tried with the other victims—at least the last two. But the killer was smart. He was either discarding or destroying their phones. Marcus had to reach Dakota before her phone was busted too. Had to reach her before *he* did.

His stomach twisted. Was he admitting she was right? The killer was still out there?

"Drat," he said, tense.

He pushed the gas pedal to the floor, hit the sirens, screeching like a banshee through the night, hastening rapidly towards the last known location of his partner. At the same time, his phone connected. The FBI came with perks. "Yes, hello. Clement. Badge number Forty-two—q—one. No, wait, yes. Urgent. I need you to track a phone. It might be off.

I need you to find where it is right now."

He picked up the speed. The darkness of night was illuminated by flashing red and blue as he tore through the outskirts of town, racing towards a desert road

CHAPTER TWENTY SEVEN

Dakota screamed. Matching the same sound from Mrs. Lopez, but also distracting the killer for a brief moment. He whirled around, knife in hand, teeth bared. "Shut up!" he spat.

She ignored this, and screamed again, a shrill, piercing sound. At this point, she just needed him to look at her.

She gave up on the saw. No way she could reach it with her hands tied. Besides, she trained as a kickboxer. Her kicks, by far her most useful asset, had made a bit of a name for her in the cage. On top of it, the killer was still underestimating her.

He sneered, waving the knife in her direction. "I'll get to you next," he snapped. "Now shut up and sit down."

She continued approaching, screaming. She wondered how it must've looked to Miranda. Another woman, small, thin, stumbling forward, screaming, hands tied, towards a man with a knife.

They must both have thought she was out of her mind. Perfect. Just what she needed.

The killer began to sneer again. He said something, but before he could finish it, she suddenly erupted.

A kick, straight to the hand. The knife went flying.

He just stared, stunned. The second kick caught him across the face. She pivoted, hands still behind her back.

She wasn't a boxer by trade. She was a fully trained mixed martial artist. Tied hands were nothing.

The killer blinked, stumbling, then blood began to drip down his nose.

"You bitch," he said, more stunned and surprised than upset.

And then he lunged for his knife.

Dakota beat him to it, kicking it away.

He howled and tried to punch her. She ducked, dodging back. He tried to punch her again. Again, she went backwards, keeping distance.

He screamed, and turned suddenly, lunging towards Miranda.

"Get on the ground, or I'll kill her," he bellowed.

He was reaching for a chisel on the nearest workbench.

But Dakota didn't give him the chance. As he dragged the chisel, and snatched at Miranda, she surged in again. Another kick, this time to the small of the back.

He stumbled forward, howling. He toppled over one of the benches.

Miranda was still tied, defenseless. Dakota still only had the use of her legs. But now, surprise was gone. The killer was snarling again, his face twisted in rage and fury. He snatched a crowbar and held it in front of him now like a shield. Tentatively, much more cautiously, his mean eyes narrowed, he approached.

Dakota tensed. A crowbar would break her shin if she wasn't careful.

"You think you're clever?" he sneered. "Don't you Mother? Don't you?" His voice was still rasping, hoarse.

Dakota frowned at him. "What did you call me?"

"I forgot. You prefer *mommy*. I hate you, Mommy!" he yelled.

The man was having a psychotic break. He was seeing someone that wasn't there. She couldn't piece it all together, but it seemed clear enough. He'd suffered at the hands of his mother's boyfriends. Or something similar. She wondered how he'd been disfigured. Now, though, wielding a crowbar, she had to focus on her own problems.

He suddenly lunged in, slamming the bar down. She jerked back. He howled and tried to slam it into her face. She ducked. He sped towards her, trying to tackle her now. This time she brought a knee up, hard. It glanced off his chin. Dazed, he stumbled past her, hitting another workbench, and this time sending it toppling to the ground. Tools scattered. What looked like an engine that he had been reassembling collapsed into six pieces. Small metal bolts went scattering.

Bleeding from his nose, sputtering, he pushed back to his feet. Dakota wished she had her hands. One blow from that crowbar and it would do serious damage. She wouldn't be able to absorb it on her forearms. If he broke a bone, it would all be over.

Tensed, breathing heavily, she backed away, trying to keep distance, hoping that cardio alone would tire him out and give her an opportunity.

"You knew I didn't know how to ride," he screamed. "You knew that he wanted me to try it." He swiped. He missed. This time she hadn't even ducked. He was erratic. Violent. He suddenly turned, charging towards Miranda. "You pretended like it wasn't his fault. It was his fault I crashed. I was only eleven!"

He slammed the crowbar towards Miranda, but Dakota lunged in, trying to block it.

But he'd been anticipating this. Almost as if this was what he'd been hoping for. He'd used Miranda as a distraction, and as Dakota came in to stop him, he whirled, bringing the crowbar down hard on her leg.

Nothing cracked. But the pain was immense. Dakota screamed, stumbling. Her leg felt funny, and she collapsed to a knee.

He cackled, and lunged in. "Stupid slut."

As he tried to bash her brain with the crowbar, she dropped to the floor. It was the only direction left to go. Flat. He missed.

He tried to stomp. She rolled. He stomped again. She rolled again.

He howled in rage and fury. "Stop moving!" he screamed.

She wasn't about to follow this request.

Another swipe of the crowbar. And another miss.

And now, rapidly, she was regaining her feet. Her shin still throbbed in agony.

She rose fully, her own anger following the ascent. Miranda was crying. A woman, successful, married, with a child, was dangling from the ceiling, bleeding and crying. And this bastard was the reason.

She couldn't let him beat her to death. She refused. She'd trained against far better fighters for much longer. She didn't even need her damn fists. She was determined now. She was gonna knock him out with just her feet.

He seemed to notice something shift in her posture. He hefted the crowbar more defensively now, waiting. He licked his lips, his tongue scraping across a particularly twisted portion of his wounded mouth.

And then she took two steps forward, lashed out, faked a kick, and followed up with a knee to his gut. The crowbar missed. He doubled over, emitting a sound like a whoopee cushion.

She was alone. He'd taken her phone. There was no backup. It was her. Or death.

High stakes. Just as she liked them.

Another kick. Another. This time, she was too fast. She didn't use her hands. Didn't need them.

He flung up his own hands to try and block his face. The crowbar fell.

Another kick.

He screamed.

This time she shoved him, sending him over the workbench again. He hit the engine and groaned. But she wasn't done. As he tried to shove to his feet, she came in, and put her full force behind the blow. Like a soccer kick, her foot caught his chin. His head snapped back. His arms flung out. He plowed to the ground, with a loud *thump*. And then went still.

Dakota breathed heavily, standing over the monster, staring down. He blinked dazedly, groaning.

"What happened?" he moaned.

She could hear the woman crying behind her. Dakota didn't hesitate. She spun, hastening towards the paint chisel he had almost used to kill Miranda. She scrambled at it with her fingers, and began cutting, slicing through strands of rope.

It was a difficult thing to maneuver the blade between the bonds behind her back. The whole time, as she finagled the precarious tool, she stared, scowling at where the killer was now sitting on the floor, weeping. He cried like a child. Tears streamed down his ruined cheeks. He wept, blubbering, shoulders shaking.

She might have felt more pity if she hadn't known what he had done to those other women. What he'd been in the middle of doing to Miranda.

And suddenly her wrists were free. She ripped the ropes, tossing them to the side, and turned, dragging a chair beneath the dangling woman, taking two steps, and then reaching for the ropes above her hands.

"Hang tight—I'm with the FBI," she murmured in what she hoped was a comforting tone into the woman's ear.

Miranda was still shaking. She nodded to show she'd heard.

Dakota cut the rope. There was no easy, gentle way to do it. Miranda fell and collapsed as her weakened legs gave out under her.

Dakota dropped from the chair, tossing the blade to the side, and quickly took a knee next the fallen woman. "Stay there. It's fine. We'll get medical. You're going to be—"

"Watch out!" Miranda screamed.

Dakota felt a faint breeze, and then a sudden painful *whack* across the back of her head. Something thick, metallic. Dazed, she stumbled.

She tried to turn and caught another blow to the back of the head. She thought she'd taken the killer down. Thought he'd given up, weeping. In her zeal to free Miranda, she hadn't taken proper precautions. She'd gotten rusty over the last few months. And now, it didn't look like it was going to matter.

He was standing over her, brandishing his helmet which he had used to bludgeon her.

Dark spots danced across her vision. She realized she was now prone. When had that happened? Her consciousness was fleeing.

She muttered, trying to speak, trying to protest. But it was no good. The killer raised his helmet, snarling, and said, "I always hated you!"

Tears still stained his cheek. Dakota heard the sound of metal scraping metal. She frowned. Was that the door?

She glimpsed a flash of shadow out of the corner of her eye. Still, she tried to regain her feet. She tried to see clearly. But the dark spots were widening.

"Die," he sneered.

The helmet came whirling down for a third, crushing blow. Miranda shouted. Dakota lost her grip against the cement, her arm buckling. And then a giant, six-foot-six pile of muscle and sinew tackled the smaller motorcycle rider from behind, like a bulldozer slamming into a bag of potatoes. Agent Marcus Clement took the Motorcycle Killer flying; the two of them soared through the air, almost majestically, in a sort of swan dive. And then they hit the ground with a sickening thump. Marcus on top. The killer below, and this time, he didn't wheeze, didn't cry. Didn't say anything. He was out cold. Marcus on top, breathing heavily. Agent Clement rounded on Dakota, eyes blazing.

He began to bellow. "Of all the stupid—"

She just said, "nice timing." And then her eyes rolled back. The black spots grew bigger and bigger. She could hear Miranda crying. But that meant the woman was alive. Silver linings. Another woman saved. She'd done it. They'd done it.

Marcus was still bellyaching. But she couldn't help but smile. Caught somewhere between consciousness and merciful sleep, Dakota just lay back, resting her head, which was bleeding, against the concrete floor. The pain didn't matter; Marcus's temper tantrum didn't matter. Miranda was alive. The killer was caught. There wasn't much more she could ask for.

CHAPTER TWENTY EIGHT

Dakota sat in the back of the ambulance. After putting so many others in the care of the paramedics over the last few days, she wasn't thrilled to now subject herself to their ministrations.

Marcus was fretting like a den mother, muttering and shaking his head and speaking in somber tones to the EMTs as they tended to her. Only two other cop cars had made it out this far on such short notice. Only one ambulance. One of the EMTs was busy darting between Dakota, sitting on the back, metal step, and Mrs. Lopez, who was on the stretcher inside the vehicle.

Others were coming, they'd assured Marcus, but were still minutes out.

Dakota didn't care, though. She'd accomplished what she'd set out to do.

The cops had placed the unconscious figure of the disfigured killer in the back seat of a squad car. The same EMT, darting back and forth between the women, was also occasionally hurrying over to the squad car, checking on the killer as well.

Dakota still thought it strange how much society went out of its way to help those who preyed on its most vulnerable.

Still, she couldn't complain.

She winced as the EMT dabbed at her head with a strong-smelling disinfectant. She winced again as he pressed a bottle of super glue against her hair line. "This is going to hurt," the man said.

Dakota tensed, teeth gritting.

As the glue was applied, and as a bandage followed, Marcus leaned in, staring down at her. His usually charming, cheerful expression was gone. He looked like someone had shot his dog as he stared at her. "What were you thinking?" he murmured beneath his breath.

Dakota blinked blearily. "It worked," she muttered.

He sighed, rubbing at the bridge of his nose. "Insane."

"Thanks."

"I mean it."

"Me too. Thanks—tracked my phone?'

"Yeah—yeah. No criminal record, by the way. Bike isn't

registered."

"I was wondering about that. Guess he just snapped."

"Yeah. I guess. But like I said... *Insane.*"

Dakota smirked. "It worked."

He sighed, closing his eyes as if against a bad dream. "You're insufferable sometimes, Steele."

She was feeling loopy. Whether from the head wound or from a successful mission, she couldn't help but grin at this.

When she did, Marcus blinked in surprise. He let out a faint, rattling breath. "Well, at least there's that."

"What?"

"That," he said more insistently. "That smile. It's been a long time, Steele. It suits your face."

She shrugged sheepishly.

"You know...," he glanced off to the squad car, his gaze moving to the back of the ambulance, then landing on Dakota. "You were right. You made the right call."

She swallowed, trying not to think too many months back to a very similar after-case debrief, with a very different tone. "Thanks," she said guarded.

"I miss this, Steele. I miss having someone I can count on. Let me be clear, though—what you did tonight was insane."

"Alright. I miss it too, Marcus."

He blinked. "You do?"

"Mhmm."

"Well... I mean... Agent Carter wasn't *too* mad about the shooting. I'm sure if—well, if you want to—"

"I'm going back to South Dakota, Marcus. I have to. There are some things I need to take care of."

Her decade-long partner looked hurt for a moment, but then he sighed and shrugged. He reached out, gently patting her on the shoulder, his enormous, mitt-sized hand draping over her arm. "Alright. I get it. I don't like it. But I get it. Thanks Steele. For helping. It means a lot."

She flashed another smile. This one wasn't as authentic as the first. But it was close.

Still, she knew what she had to do. She was telling the truth. She had to return to South Dakota.

***

But she wouldn't stay for long—she'd decided that much. Nearly a day had passed since she'd spoken last to Agent Clement. The plane ride back had been somewhat uncomfortable, due to the bouncing and jouncing and the bandage across the back of her head striking a particularly rough headrest.

Now, though, standing in her old, claustrophobic apartment, Dakota let out a faint sigh. She heard movement behind her and glanced back towards where her old mentor, Coach Little, was leaning against this walking stick.

"That everything?" he asked, glancing towards the potted plant in one hand and her suitcase in the other.

Dakota sighed, glancing back towards her apartment. Empty now. Bare. It had taken all of two hours to pack all her earthly possessions. That said something about a soul, though she wasn't sure what.

"The boys load the taxi?" she asked.

Coach Little snorted. "Those gym rats will do what I say. Unlike some I know," he added, giving her a significant glance.

She smiled, hefted the orchid flowerpot and adjusted her grip on her packed suitcase.

"You got the keys?" she said.

Coach Little wiggled the apartment key, the metal flashing where it dangled from his extended finger. She emitted another melancholy sigh, but then nodded determinedly. She'd already committed. She'd known what she had to do. Had known the moment Marcus asked her. Had known the moment she'd seen Mrs. Lopez still alive.

People needed her out there. She wasn't doing any good for anyone locked inside this apartment. Besides, saving lives was intoxicating. It was the best rush she'd felt in a while. She needed the job just as much as people needed her.

"You sure you got everything?" Little said.

She paused, staring in the direction of the bathroom. She thought of the bottle she'd emptied in the sink. Her throat itched. Part of her wanted to go and check, just to make sure.

She felt an itch in the middle of her spine. Determinedly, she turned away. "Yeah—that's everything."

She hooked the door with the back of her foot and pulled it shut.

As she did, Coach Little inserted the key in the lock, securing the door. Dakota hefted her favorite orchid plant. A small, green bud had formed from where she'd pruned it. No petals, no flower yet, but a bud. Another looked like it was pushing through the stem.

She stared at the orchid briefly, blinking.

"This place is month-to-month, yeah?" Little asked.

Dakota smiled, looking away from her plant and nodding. She began to wheel her suitcase, moving towards the stairs. She waited patiently as her coach hobbled after her, tossing and catching the key spryly.

"Just dump it in the landlord's box," she said. "Or I'll switch you. Take the plant, I'll deal with the key."

Casper waved away the offer. "Forget the key, Dakota. You sure you want to leave again without seeing *him*?"

Dakota paused, wincing at the comment. Of course, she didn't want to see her father. Not now. Not after all these years. No—no, she'd made up her mind. She was cutting ties. She was returning to Quantico. Marcus would be ecstatic.

But also, it was the last real shot at life she had. She couldn't blow it.

"I'm sure," she murmured softly.

She paused as they circled the stairs and glanced out towards the curb where the taxi was waiting. The final few possessions she had were now in the trunk of the car, deposited by two of Casper's trainees from the gym. The boys, in tracksuits, leaned against the yellow cab, ignoring the driver's nervous glances.

Dakota rolled her eyes, wheeling her suitcase down the steps.

"You're gonna be alright out there, yeah?" Casper said, strolling along next to her and still tossing and catching the keys. "Won't need me to come break any legs I hope."

"I mean... I might need *some* legs broken," Dakota said. She winced. "Especially with the drug tests."

"Right... So what's the deal with that again?"

Dakota sighed, shaking her head as they rounded the banister. "Once a month. Agent Carter *insisted.*" She shivered, remembering the phone call from the previous night on the airplane. She wasn't one to beg, but it had almost felt like that was what Supervising Agent Carter had wanted in order to allow Dakota a second shot.

Then again, she hadn't been able to argue with results.

They'd caught the Motorcycle Murderer.

At least Carter seemed to respect solved cases.

"Drug-testing. I mean, you've peed in a cup before." Coach Little shrugged. "All fighters have."

"Yeah," she said with a sigh as they reached the bottom floor, and she watched as Little deposited the apartment key in the mail slot for the landlord's unit 1A.

The slot made the satisfying, metallic *clicking* sound as it shut once more. That done, Dakota almost felt lighter. She hadn't had a drink in two days, and yet it didn't hurt so much. Coach Little reached out, taking her suitcase from her, despite her protest, and strolled casually alongside, moving towards the front door.

"It's the therapy I'm worried about," Dakota muttered. "Never been to therapy. Sounds like kook stuff."

The Irishman nodded sympathetically. "Kook stuff for sure."

Part of her wondered if she was making a mistake. The apartment wasn't so bad, was it? It was comfortable. The dark, dingy unit had swaddled her. Protected her in a way.

All of this new stuff: no more drinking, a promise to visit a therapist twice a month... And that didn't include the high-demanding Quantico hours and cases.

Was she really ready for this?

She'd felt so certain on the plane. Felt so certain after their collar. But now...

Part of her wanted to sprint back up the stairs, hide inside her unit and never come out again.

"Hey champ," Casper murmured from where he waited on the sidewalk just outside the door. "Taxi is waiting."

She turned to face him, swallowing. She let out a shaking gust of air.

"You good?" he said.

She bit her lip. Then answered honestly. "I'm scared."

He nodded without missing a beat. "Good," he said. "Means you're smart." He smiled and winked. "I ain't never seen quit in Tastee yet."

She sighed, forcing a smirk. "You know I hate that name, right?"

"Known it for ten years, dear. Never stopped me once. Now come on—he's gonna drive away with your stuff if you don't hurry."

Dakota smiled, this time authentically and stepped out of the apartment building, allowing the door to swing shut behind her. Her chest pounded. Her palms prickled. But as she moved, she picked up her pace, hastening towards the front seat of the waiting cab.

She nodded in gratitude towards Casper's two students, and they both nodded back, pushing off their reclining positions on the cab.

She paused at the front door of the taxi as the gym-rats helped load her suitcase. She kept the orchid pot in her hand. She liked looking at it, even without the flowers.

"Dakota," Casper said.

"Coach?"

"You're going to do fine. You know that, don't you?"

She looked at him as she slid into the front seat, next to the driver who was still shooting suspicious glances in the mirrors while tracking the two boxers. She said, "I hope so."

"Hope is good. But listen to me. I'm telling you. You'll do great, kid. You always do. You're a champ, got me? We all root for you. All of us back here. Don't hesitate to stop by if you need anything...," he paused, reconsidering, then held up a finger. "Well, if you're just coming to quit and wallow, then you might as well skip town."

Dakota snorted. "Great to know. No more wallowing in Rapid City. Gotcha. Well—I'd be dead without you, Coach." She said this with a shrug. No smile, no sarcasm. Just a bare fact. Sometimes those had to be communicated. Remembered.

And it was true. Without Casper, she easily could've still been living on the streets. Or not living at all.

She wasn't sure what different crossroads led to. Wasn't sure what awaited down one path or another. Sometimes, it felt like she chose well. Other times it felt like she didn't choose at all.

Her coach gave her a wink and a quick pat on the back. Then, so he wouldn't look too weak in front of the boys, he snapped, "Now get your ass in gear, Tastee. You're wasting daylight." He slammed the door for her, his eyes twinkling, and watched from the curb as the driver hastily pulled away.

"Regional airport," Dakota said at a quick questioning glance.

She settled in her seat, buckling slowly, the orchid pot resting on her lap. Only a single bud, a single glimpse of life sprouting from the pruned deadwood.

Therapy, a new supervising agent... Dakota shivered at the thought of it. But when she considered the look on Marcus's face when she arrived in Quantico...

She grinned now, sitting a bit straighter.

Agent Clement's reaction alone would make it worth it. She'd missed her partner. She knew that now.

Dakota settled, staring through the windshield as the taxi driver took her to the airport. As they picked up speed, her brow furrowed. Another thought cycled through her mind—the one she hadn't told anyone. The one she was keeping just for herself. She wanted to return to Quantico, wanted to help solve cases again. Wanted to work with

Marcus.

But also...

She closed her eyes, picturing the still, lifeless body permanently etched into the inside of her eyelids. *I'm the wind...*

He thought he'd gotten away.

Thought he'd dodged her. He was in the wind, hiding, gone, gone...

For now.

But she was determined. Coach Little had been right—she wasn't a quitter. Not with anything. She wasn't going to start now.

Besides... she'd already taken the first step. She lifted her phone and stared.

A new voicemail.

She swallowed, her fingers shaking.

She'd saved the number as SAD. Supervising Agent Drafuss. Her old field office head. She'd deleted his number months ago but had gotten it again from Marcus. She'd placed a voicemail of her own after the plane ride.

She hadn't expected him to get back to her so soon.

She shot a look towards the driver, turning the volume down and pressing the device to her cheek so only she could hear.

She hadn't told the others the *entire* reason she was taking her old job back.

Only Drafuss knew... He'd been in charge when the killer had escaped three months ago. He'd tracked every detail of the case.

Dakota felt a jolt of apprehension as she listened.

But slowly, listening to the tone of the recorded voice, her excitement slipped. Her scowl returned.

"...Not a chance in hell, Steele," the recorded message started. *"It's a dead case. Got me? Don't call again..."*

For a moment, she thought it had ended there.

But then, with a quick gulp of air like a sailboat gathering wind, the old supervisor continued, louder on the recorded message. *"...this wasn't just about you, Steele! Shit. Just let it go, okay? The case is dead. Dead. Dead. He got away. Just let it go. I mean it—lose my number again, will you? You did fine, Steele. Letting him slip was probably the best thing anyway. There are things going on here... Things you and Marcus never knew. Just—just* please." To her astonishment, his voice cracked. With fear? Grief?

"Let it go!" he said a final time.

And then the message ended. The voicemail chirped something to her about replaying the message. Dakota lowered her phone slowly, clicking the button to save the strange recording.

Something had Drafuss spooked. Scared?

No. Not scared.

Terrified.

There was terror in that man's voice.

Which only left one question—why was a seasoned FBI agent so scared?

They'd dealt with killers before. All the time. Serial or otherwise. This wasn't the first cold case.

But it was the first time she'd ever hit such a stone wall of resistance.

She stared at her phone, half-wondering if she ought to call Drafuss right then and there. She bit her lip and then dialed the number, raising her phone.

Straight to voicemail.

She dialed again.

The same.

Dialed again. Nothing.

He was dodging her now. The phone was off.

Dakota wrinkled her nose, staring at the phone. What was he so scared of? What was in those case files she'd requested that he wouldn't want her to see, anyway? She'd written half those reports, hadn't she?

The killer who'd escaped three months ago thought he'd outsmarted them. And maybe he had. But he would have to do it again and again and again. As long as Dakota had breath, the killer wouldn't have rest. And eventually... he'd make a mistake.

Once he did, she'd be waiting there for him.

So no, she wasn't about to quit now.

If anything, she'd only just started.

She frowned at the phone, more confused than concerned. Was something else going on here?

She lifted the device, staring at it. And then she played the scared voicemail once again, listening to each and every word and trying to read between the lines. The more her old boss insisted she stay away, the more certain Dakota was that she'd kick over every damn stone to see what wriggled beneath.

And this one...

She hadn't taken the time to pay attention. She'd been so caught up in her own failure.

But this one was a wriggler.

She listened to the voicemail, intently, her brow darkening with each stuttered, panicked word.

NOW AVAILABLE!

WITHOUT REMORSE

(A Dakota Steele FBI Suspense Thriller—Book 2)

MMA champ-turned-FBI Special Agent and BAU specialist Dakota Steele is as tough as they come—and as brilliant, too, able to crack serial killers that no one else can. But when bodies turn up in scrap metal yards, displayed in dramatic and disturbing ways, Dakota may have finally met her match.

"The plot has many twists and turns, but it is the ending, which I did not see coming at all, that totally defines this book as one of the most riveting that I have read in years."
—Reader review for Not Like Us

WITHOUT REMORSE is book #2 in a brand new series by critically-acclaimed and #1 bestselling mystery and suspense author Ava Strong.

As the case grows more complex, leading down a maze of dead ends, Dakota realizes there may be one clue just out of reach. And after a shocking twist, Dakota realizes that this killer may not be who she thinks he is. He may just be far more diabolical.

Yet Dakota must still battle her own demons—the disappearance of her sister, the estrangement of her father—as all of it bears down on her at once.

Can she hold it together long enough to solve the case?

Or will the trauma of her past threaten to swallow her for good?

A complex psychological crime thriller full of twists and turns and packed with heart-pounding suspense, the DAKOTA STEELE mystery series will make you fall in love with a brilliant new female protagonist and keep you turning pages late into the night.

Book #3 in the series—WITHOUT A PAST—is now also available.

Ava Strong

Bestselling author Ava Strong is author of the REMI LAURENT mystery series, comprising six books (and counting); of the ILSE BECK mystery series, comprising seven books (and counting); of the STELLA FALL psychological suspense thriller series, comprising six books (and counting); and of the DAKOTA STEELE FBI Suspense thriller series, comprising three books (and counting).

An avid reader and lifelong fan of the mystery and thriller genres, Ava loves to hear from you, so please feel free to visit www.avastrongauthor.com to learn more and stay in touch.

BOOKS BY AVA STRONG

REMI LAURENT FBI SUSPENSE THRILLER
THE DEATH CODE (Book #1)
THE MURDER CODE (Book #2)
THE MALICE CODE (Book #3)
THE VENGEANCE CODE (Book #4)
THE DECEPTION CODE (Book #5)
THE SEDUCTION CODE (Book #6)

ILSE BECK FBI SUSPENSE THRILLER
NOT LIKE US (Book #1)
NOT LIKE HE SEEMED (Book #2)
NOT LIKE YESTERDAY (Book #3)
NOT LIKE THIS (Book #4)
NOT LIKE SHE THOUGHT (Book #5)
NOT LIKE BEFORE (Book #6)
NOT LIKE NORMAL (Book #7)

STELLA FALL PSYCHOLOGICAL SUSPENSE THRILLER
HIS OTHER WIFE (Book #1)
HIS OTHER LIE (Book #2)
HIS OTHER SECRET (Book #3)
HIS OTHER MISTRESS (Book #4)
HIS OTHER LIFE (Book #5)
HIS OTHER TRUTH (Book #6)

DAKOTA STEELE FBI SUSPENSE THRILLER
WITHOUT MERCY (Book #1)
WITHOUT REMORSE (Book #2)
WITHOUT A PAST (Book #3)

www.ingramcontent.com/pod-product-compliance
Lightning Source LLC
Chambersburg PA
CBHW030616310726
48979CB00003B/737

* 9 7 8 1 0 9 4 3 9 4 9 9 2 *